Sins of the Saints

In this collection of stories by ex-Mormon author Johnny Townsend, we see a missionary cope with the startling discovery his companion has been translated off the face of the Earth. A teenage girl pretends to be her brother so she can "hold the priesthood" for at least a day.

A young man taught that loved ones watch over family members from the Other Side keeps imagining his grandmother catching him masturbating. A former prostitute, now a faithful Latter-day Saint, finds that some of her fellow congregants can't get beyond her past. A schizophrenic Single Adult leads a secret life no one in her congregation suspects.

Praise for Johnny Townsend

In *Zombies for Jesus,* "Townsend isn't writing satire, but deeply emotional and revealing portraits of people who are, with a few exceptions, quite lovable."

Kel Munger, *Sacramento News and Review*

In *Sex among the Saints,* "Townsend writes with a deadpan wit and a supple, realistic prose that's full of psychological empathy….he takes his protagonists' moral struggles seriously and invests them with real emotional resonance."

Kirkus Reviews

Inferno in the French Quarter: The UpStairs Lounge Fire is "a gripping account of all the horrors that transpired that night, as well as a respectful remembrance of the victims."

Terry Firma, Patheos

"Johnny Townsend's 'Partying with St. Roch' [in the anthology *Latter-Gay Saints*] tells a beautiful, haunting tale."

Kent Brintnall, Out in Print: Queer Book Reviews

Selling the City of Enoch is "sharply intelligent…pleasingly complex…The stories are full of…doubters, but there's no vindictiveness in these pages; the characters continuously poke holes in Mormonism's more extravagant absurdities, but they take very little pleasure in doing so….Many of Townsend's stories…have a provocative edge to them, but this [book] displays a great deal of insight as well…a playful, biting and surprisingly warm collection."

Kirkus Reviews

Gayrabian Nights is "an allegorical tour de force…a hard-core emotional punch."

Gay. Guy. Reading and Friends

The Washing of Brains has "A lovely writing style, and each story [is] full of unique, engaging characters….immensely entertaining."

Rainbow Awards

In *Dead Mankind Walking*, "Townsend writes in an energetic prose that balances crankiness and humor….A rambunctious volume of short, well-crafted essays…"

Kirkus Reviews

Sins of the Saints

Johnny Townsend

Contents

The Day My Sister Held the Priesthood.....................9
That Time the Single Adults in My Ward All
        Decided They Wanted to Be Murdered...............28
The Translation of Elder Bauman..........................39
Casting the Last Stone...................................48
Secret Agent of the Esplanade Ward.......................60
The Media Fast...68
The Tree of Li(f)e.......................................82
The Organ Donor..94
To Serve Man..105
Exit Interview..115
The Merit Badge...125
Faith-Promoting Faith...................................145
Grandma Is a Slutty Perv................................159
Garbage Everywhere......................................175
The Dissociative Singularity of the Gods................189
Foreseeing the Future...................................211
Books by Johnny Townsend................................228
What Readers Have Said..................................241

The Day My Sister Held the Priesthood

"Family council!" There was a loud bang on my bedroom door. A string of Christmas lights I'd hung up to make the place more festive rattled in protest. "Everyone in the living room now!" Dad moved on to my sister's room down the hall and pounded on her door as well.

Pam and I joined our parents in the living room a few moments later. Dad sat in his easy chair, as usual. Mom sat on the ottoman. Pam and I sat on the sofa. Christmas tree ornaments in the shape of various temples hung from our freshly cut fir.

"What's up?" I asked.

"Opening prayer first, Brian," Dad said. He pointed at Mom, and she folded her arms and bowed her head, the rest of us following suit. After our synchronized amens, Dad smiled broadly at my sister and me. "I have good news. You guys are going to be so excited."

Pam and I exchanged glances. I couldn't imagine what might be up. We never went on vacation. Dad had made it clear years ago we were never going to move away from this house. And it seemed unlikely we were getting a new brother or sister at this point, something we'd hoped for over the years. Someone to deflect attention from us.

Pam and I were sixteen, fraternal twins obviously, and our parents had decided shortly after we were born that they would give the rest of the kids assigned them during the Pre-Existence their physical bodies during the Millennium. It was too hard and too spiritually risky to take care of them in today's world.

Mom faced some disapproval from the other sisters in the ward, but she was quite firm, perhaps the only time in her life. Though Dad didn't have to change any diapers, he did still hear us wail. They didn't want a passel of kids.

Was that the correct term, I wondered? There was a gaggle of geese, a pride of lions, a murder of crows. When Mom related the story of her rebellion each year on our birthday, she might as well have been using the phrase "a misery of children."

I didn't think Pam and I were that bad. We didn't wail anymore, anyway. Pam got detention at school once in a while, but she was never suspended. And I was often the teacher's pet. Our parents could've done worse in the children department. As it turned out, limiting the number of their offspring was the only rebellious act they ever committed. In every other way, they were as Mormon as you could come.

"The Church just announced that priests can now perform baptisms for the dead in the temple." Dad's smile grew even broader. "And Laurels can now hand out towels."

A stunned silence filled the room, broken finally by my sister saying, "You've got to be kidding." She sighed in frustration. "Brian gets to save souls and *I* get to deal with the linens?"

"Oh, Pam," Mom said softly, "you know the role of women is to support the men."

Pam turned to me and I blushed.

"Now you guys can go to the temple every month like adults do," Dad continued. "Maybe even more. So we'll need to have our father-son and father-daughter interviews every week to keep you worthy."

I didn't dare turn to see Pam's reaction to this. We both hated those infernal interviews, which presently occurred once a month, on Fast Sunday.

"We'll do the interviews right after church each week. But since we're all here together right now, I just want to emphasize again to Pam that you're *never* to 'hold the priesthood.'"

I snickered. "Holding the priesthood" was Dad's euphemism for hand jobs. "Passing spit" was the term he used for kissing, and "descending on Mary" was how he phrased intercourse.

He'd say things like, "Brian, I don't want you to see Judi again. I've seen her at church wearing sleeveless tops. With that kind of temptation, you'll end up descending on Mary before long."

You'd think he might at least substitute the name of the actual girl in question. I personally didn't understand what all the hoopla was over exposed shoulders. I found practically any girl, modestly dressed or not, easy to fantasize about. As far as Pam giving a guy a hand job, my parents had worried for years that because she was such a tomboy she might end up lesbian.

Since she'd turned sixteen, though, and could now legally date, she went out with the wildest boys in the ward, the bishop's son and the son of the second counselor in the stake presidency. I wondered if our folks ever considered that Pam might be better off if she was dating someone like Judi.

Judi passed spit quite well. She also liked to go on and on about her needlepoint. But a tongueful of spit easily made up for that.

"That goes for you, too, young man," Dad said, turning to me. "No holding your own priesthood, either."

I could hear Pam snickering now.

Thankfully, the family council was disbanded for the day after a few more comments, these about how good it was to be living in the fulness of times. The closing prayer was assigned to Pam, and then we were done.

My sister and I walked back to our rooms quietly. I had taped a poster of Temple Square in Salt Lake all decorated in holiday lights on my door. Pam's door was completely bare. Back in my room, I picked up my Geometry book and tried to memorize another theorem. I could hear Pam turning up the music in her room.

It wasn't "Deck the Halls." She usually used headphones, except when she was upset, so it was clear she hadn't been inspired by Dad's news. I'd have to go talk to her later. I could always calm her down, just as she could always calm me. It was true what they said about twins. We had a connection.

We'd been close from the very beginning, according to Mom, rarely fighting even as toddlers. Growing up, Pam usually sported a short, boyish haircut. We looked so much alike that we sometimes pretended to be each other when the fancy struck us. Dad was always upset when we revealed our deception, afraid I'd end up a "transvestite," but I never had to wear a dress on the occasions I impersonated Pam since she only wore them on Sunday.

There was that one time, of course, when I came close. Not long after I'd been ordained a deacon, Pam asked if she could pass the sacrament some Sunday. "It's not as if I'm blessing it," she said. "It'll already have been blessed. You don't really need the priesthood just to pass it around the chapel. It's not an actual ordinance. There's no reason girls couldn't be doing it now."

She had a point, and one Sunday when Dad was out of town and Mom was home sick, Pam and I made the switch. Well, she made the switch. I still wasn't willing to wear a dress to become a Beehive for the day. We both left the house as boys, and I waited down the street from the ward meetinghouse for Pam to come back.

No one ever discovered it was my sister carrying the trays of bread and water that day along with the real deacons. But we'd never done another switch since then. The older we got, the more our faces started to diverge, though sometimes when one of the distant aunts and uncles came to visit, they still couldn't tell us apart at first.

But then, Aunt Beatrice had long suffered trouble with her eyesight. She'd once gone to the eye doctor about her cataracts. The doctor removed her glasses, cleaned them, and instructed her to put them back on. Problem solved.

But she didn't seem to remember this simple remedy and let her glasses get dirty again, so perhaps it wasn't that much of an accomplishment to fool her. These days, Pam's haircut was close to but not exactly like mine. I still only had a light fuzz on my cheeks, and Pam was not quite as busty as Dale would have liked. We dressed pretty much the same way, in jeans and solid color button-down shirts made of thick cotton, except on Sunday, the only time either of us dressed up.

After I worked on my Geometry another hour, I let myself think about the new opportunity the Church was providing. The youth had long frequented the temple to be dunked by temple workers. Usually, one waited in line for maybe an hour with a horde of other teenagers—was it a disaster of teens?—in our white jumpsuits and then each spent perhaps a minute and a half in the font being baptized over and over in rapid succession for fifteen people who had died and were waiting in Spirit Prison for us to do their work for them.

After being ordained a priest by my father on my sixteenth birthday, I technically had the authority to baptize converts and to marry couples. Live ones, anyway. But in reality, teenage Mormon priests hardly ever performed either of these ordinances.

To be honest, even most missionaries rarely had the chance to baptize actual people these days. The world was growing too wicked to recognize the truth anymore. I suspected this policy change was to try to encourage the youth to become stronger in the gospel, so they wouldn't fall away like so many of the Single Adults did.

Judi's older brother went inactive right after coming home from his mission. Judi kept asking me if I thought she should talk to him anymore. I kept saying yes, but she kept asking. I wasn't sure if she was hoping I'd change my mind or if she was hoping I'd find a way to finally convince her.

The music softened in Pam's room, so I didn't head over to talk to her. There were times when we knew to give each other space. But those times were rare. Back when she'd experienced her first several periods, Pam had forced me to look at her bloodied pads. She felt it was important as her twin to have at least a minimal appreciation of what she went through every month. It was eye opening, to be sure, but it didn't make me want to know any deeper female secrets.

On my third date with Judi, though, when she mentioned it was her time of the month, I put my hand on hers and said bravely, "Did you want to show me your pads?" It turned out that this show of solidarity did not have the desired effect of bringing us closer together. Two more months passed before she would go out with me again.

I finished studying my Geometry for the evening and then read a couple of chapters from the Pearl of Great Price. I got down on my knees and prayed for Heavenly Father to keep me worthy so I could work in the temple. And go on a mission. And marry Judi or some other nice girl for time and eternity. And make it to the Celestial Kingdom with her.

It was difficult to ever think of just the immediate future. As a Mormon, I felt the weight of thousands of millennia on my shoulders every day.

The next morning in Seminary, Pam looked distracted and proved she wasn't paying attention to our teacher when he asked her a question and she didn't even hear him. Dale, the bishop's son, gave her a thumbs up, but she didn't notice that, either.

Judi flashed me a look of concern. She always considered my sister to be a little unorthodox and refused to socialize too closely with her. So I decided to pull Pam aside when class was over.

"What's up, Sis?"

"Brian," she whispered, "I've got a plan."

I frowned. The last time she'd said that, she sneaked off to Starbucks to try her first coffee while she sent me to buy a packet of mints to disguise her breath. I wasn't pleased at her violation of the Word of Wisdom, but we stuck up for each other no matter what.

Fortunately, she hated the taste, and that was that. Pot was legal now, however, and I dreaded the day that would surely come when Pam asked me to help her buy brownies. I hoped she'd wait till she was eighteen and I was away on my mission. I tried to guess what else she might be planning today but couldn't think of anything.

"I'm going to hold the priesthood."

Instinctively, one of my hands moved to protect my crotch. My eyebrows furrowed.

"You'll go do baptisms in the temple a couple of times. Then you'll tell me whatever I need to know that I can't see for myself while I hand out towels."

"Pam..."

"Then we'll switch temple recommends, and I'll go in and perform the baptisms just for one session."

My mouth fell open.

"I know those baptisms won't count," Pam added quickly, "but the recorders will keep track of who does which baptism, and they can always redo those later."

"Pam..."

"We're not really hurting any spirits."

"This isn't like passing the sacrament..."

"It's not fair, Brian. Boys get to do everything. All I get to do is bake cookies and fold laundry."

It was impossible to know my sister for sixteen years and be unaware of her ideas about equality. I wasn't sure it was possible to be a teenager in our society and not feel she was probably right. We knew all about the "roles" Heavenly Father had foreordained—the Proclamation on the Family was hanging on our living room wall—but my Geometry teacher was every bit as smart as my Civics teacher.

What did it matter that one was a man and the other a woman? And the male cafeteria workers at school seemed every bit as capable at making mashed potatoes as the women.

Pam and I talked secretly sometimes about how we expected the Church to grant women the priesthood during our lifetime, the way it had eventually come around and granted Blacks the priesthood in 1978. I was willing to wait for the Lord's timetable to unroll naturally, but Pam was growing increasingly impatient.

Sometimes, when she recounted some of the things the bishop said during their interviews, she'd conclude with, "When *I'm* a bishop one day..." Of course, she never finished that sentence.

But now…

"I know we still look a lot alike," I began, "but—"

"I've got Keira Knightly breasts," Pam interrupted, "and I'll wrap them down. I'll go in wearing your suit. No one will be expecting a girl, so they won't look hard enough to check."

"You'll have to change clothes in the men's dressing room."

"That's nothing. If I have to, I can change in the toilet stall."

"What if you get caught?"

"When was the last time you heard of a sixteen-year-old being excommunicated?"

"We might always be the first."

The idea seemed to intrigue Pam rather than worry her. She shrugged. "So I'll repent and be baptized again a year later. I'll let you do the baptism."

"Unless they ex me, too, as a co-conspirator."

Over the next couple of weeks, as Christmas came and went, I thought a lot about what Pam had said, and we talked about her plan again and again. Christmas helped me make up my mind. Dad gave me a hunting knife, as if I'd ever use such a thing, and Mom gave Pam a cookbook of *Pioneer Recipes*, something she wasn't likely to use very often, either.

But the important thing, the essential thing, was that the gifts were "appropriate." I went to the temple just before New Year's to perform baptisms for my first time, discovering that I was both excited and terrified at doing so. The prayer itself was short and easy to memorize, but I was still afraid to louse it up, that the other teens I dunked wouldn't go all the way under and I'd have to dunk them again.

I wasn't prepared for the discovery that I'd have to dunk teenage girls as well as boys. I hoped I wouldn't get a boner. It would be painfully obvious in my wet, clinging pants as I climbed out of the font.

What also turned out to be painfully obvious were the breasts on every girl I dunked, as their jumpsuits clung to them the way I wanted to. Thank goodness Judi wasn't one of the girls in line. I realized that Pam was right at least about this. It would be better for a girl to baptize other girls.

I did end up getting the boner, naturally. After I met my baptism quota, I took a deep breath when it was time to climb out of the font, a little miffed I wasn't allowed the necessary time to debone before exiting. Pam covered her mouth and snickered.

As a teenager, I often experienced erections popping up at the most inconvenient of times. Under normal circumstances, I could close my eyes and bring up an image of a willow tree in my mind, with its long, limp branches. I'd concentrate on those drooping branches for a few minutes until I grew flaccid.

But there was really no opportunity to do that now. At least I could use the towel as a shield once the towel girl handed it to me. And the towel girl wasn't Pam. We seemed to have trouble synchronizing our volunteer schedules at the font. But that was just as well, as it allowed Pam to concentrate fully on observing exactly what I was doing.

In the dressing room, adult men were changing into their whites—were they a bleaching of temple workers?—to guide others through an endowment ceremony for the folks who'd had their baptisms done. Then at some point, someone else would take care of their proxy marriages. I wasn't sure if the ordinances had to be performed chronologically to count, or if the spirit in question could just wait till everything had been done and then accept the whole package at one time.

After my third time at the font near the end of January, Pam cornered me in a stairwell. "I think I know what to do," she said, describing everything she'd witnessed over the past month. "Did I miss anything?"

"Wear an extra T-shirt," I said. "You don't want the band around your breasts to show through."

"Already got it covered."

Fast Sunday was that weekend, and I fasted to know if Heavenly Father was okay with our deception, which seemed an order of magnitude higher than our last. Since I didn't hear him say he had anything against it, I scheduled another round of baptisms the next Saturday, the tenth of February.

Judi's birthday was two days after that. I'd have to come up with something special to connect it to Valentine's Day or risk another long hiatus from dating.

Pam and I didn't tell Mom and Dad we were going to the temple, saying instead we were going to see a movie. Otherwise, one of them would've had to drive us down. We still had to sneak out of the house, though, so they wouldn't see us all dressed up. We knew *they'd* be able to tell us apart. We walked a couple of blocks and then called a cab to take us the rest of the way.

I felt like a fool, my first time in a dress. I even had to shave my legs. What a thoroughly annoying requirement for womanhood. Why girls put up with that, I didn't know. Pam kept looking at me as I drew the razor over my shins, snickering and shaking her head.

I thought it rude, considering I was the one sacrificing for her. I was amazed, though, how much she looked like me while dressed in my blue suit. Her lips were a little thinner than mine, and our ears weren't quite the same, but most people didn't pay attention to ears. And those who did weren't likely to remember who had which ears.

I know I blushed when I handed Pam's recommend to the volunteer at the front desk. Her eyes narrowed a little, but

I expect she just thought I had some unresolved sin in my life and didn't feel worthy to enter. She didn't press the issue, though, and I moved on and let Pam hand the woman my recommend. Pam was as calm as Abinadi talking to King Noah, and a moment later, we headed for the dressing rooms. I wore a padded bra because I couldn't very well let any girls or women see my breastless chest.

I kept my eyes completely to myself while I put on my jumpsuit. A boner at this point, obviously, would give the whole thing away. I think I was so nervous I wouldn't have gotten an erection anyway, so maybe the precautions were unnecessary, but I also felt it would be rude to look when they didn't know I was a guy, so I didn't.

Most of the teens today appeared to be here on a temple trip from out of town. I recognized a couple from regional activities, but I didn't engage anyone in conversation. Pam had explained the procedure for becoming towel girl—it didn't sound difficult—and before long, I stood next to the font beside a table stacked high with white towels. I looked down at the twelve oxen, holding no priesthood authority themselves but still essential to the ordinance. At least in this temple. Not all temple fonts had such oxen, which seemed a shame.

I had to wait almost twenty minutes before it was Pam's turn to officiate. It seemed more boys were taking advantage of the new rules than girls, which surprised me a little as girls were generally more spiritual than we were. But I supposed the thrill of passing out towels wasn't enough to compete with normal Saturday activities. So the girls' shifts were longer than those of the boys.

Of course, boys might start dropping out too once the thrill of accepting new responsibilities got old.

Finally, though, after just a little more waiting, Pam approached, a bit too slowly for a full display of confidence. But again, no one challenged her. She stepped into the font and looked up at me with a smile. I suddenly wanted to shout. "Bend with your knees! Be careful not to get your chest wet when you dunk everyone!" But the time for advice was over.

And then the first teenager joined her in the font. A boy about fourteen. He looked utterly bored, probably forced to come against his will. That happened to a lot of the kids from church. Pam arranged their hands and arms in the proper fashion, took a deep breath, and said the prayer. She made her voice huskier than normal, but she still didn't sound like me. My heart began racing.

Pam immersed the boy and then helped him upright once more. The boy wiped his eyes and took another breath before Pam recited the prayer again, this time "for and in behalf of" the next dead man on her list. I heard that baptisms had been done both for Anne Frank and Hitler. But the Jewish community had insisted Anne's baptism be revoked.

It seemed odd to think Hitler might be Mormon in the next world and Anne Frank would end up the one damned.

The fourteen-year-old boy choked on some water, and Pam had to wait a moment while he regained his breath. She dunked the young man fifteen times altogether. Then he climbed the steps to leave the font.

Pam turned to me with a grin, her eyes shouting, "We did it!"

Several more boys followed, and then an irreverent string of teenage girls—a giggle of girls?—went into the font one after another. I remembered hearing that the dead hovered over these ordinances, excited to finally have their rites. I wondered if they were screaming at the recorder right now, and if the recorder was worthy enough to hear it.

He seemed oblivious, thank goodness.

Before we knew it, Pam's time was up. She climbed out of the font, I handed her a towel, and then I watched as she headed back to the dressing room. I still had to play towel girl another fifteen minutes before I could head back to the dressing rooms myself. I put Pam's dress back on and waited for her in the lobby, surprised she wasn't already there ahead of me.

My heart began beating faster again. Had she been caught? Was she being interrogated by the temple president? Was he calling our parents this very second? What if we were grounded for six months? I couldn't bear not seeing Judi outside of church for that long. My father already insisted I see her no more than once a month.

It was excruciating to know she was dating other boys on other weekends, but I knew Dad was right. I didn't want anything to keep me away from serving as a missionary.

Something like the excommunication that loomed over my head today.

A moment later, Pam showed up, and we walked calmly out of the building. At least, we tried to appear calm. I was sure anyone within a ten-foot radius could hear my pounding heart. I was anxious to quiz Pam on her experience as a priest, but we kept walking a couple of blocks to make sure no other temple-goers had followed and might overhear us or catch on at the last minute somehow as they drove past.

"So?" I demanded.

Pam shrugged. "Well, I finally held the priesthood for the first time."

"And how was it?"

"No, Brian, I mean I *held the priesthood.*"

I frowned.

"In the locker room, there was a boy with an erection."

"Oh, no."

"Another boy pointed and started making fun, and the first boy began swaggering and saying he was going to beat off in the temple, and what did the other boy think about that?"

"How awful for you!"

Pam shook her head. "No," she said slowly. "I felt grown up somehow after what I'd just done in the baptistry, so I pointed toward a bathroom stall. The two boys grinned, and all three of us squeezed in."

"Pam!" While part of me was surprised, another part wasn't. I knew Judi would never have done such a thing. Judi wouldn't even watch PG-13 movies. They had to be G or regular PG. We'd even fought over it on a couple of occasions.

It struck me for the first time that just because I knew my sister quite well, I didn't necessarily know what all women were like. Pam was clearly her own person, and I might be more successful with Judi if I recognized Judi was her own person, too.

She shrugged again. "Haven't you ever wanted to know what girls do when no guys are around?"

"You don't masturbate together, do you!?"

Pam laughed. "Of course not, but we *do* behave differently when we feel safe away from you guys."

I nodded, feeling curious about what I might be missing. "So what happened next?"

"They started playing with themselves and encouraged me to whip mine out as well." She paused. I wasn't sure that sounded as "grown up" as Pam thought. I remembered doing similar things in the Boy Scouts when I was twelve. "But I reached over and grabbed the first boy's penis, and..."

"He let you!?"

"Seemed to like it."

"Oh my god, Pam!"

My sister smiled. "You shouldn't take the Lord's name in vain."

I stared at her for a couple of minutes, unable to come up with anything in response. Finally, I managed, "You're going to have to confess to the bishop now." When the whole story came out, I'd be implicated, too. But I'd suffer whatever punishment was meted out if it helped my sister.

Pam turned to look back toward the temple. We could still see its spire towering over the houses in the neighborhood. "I want to bless the sacrament tomorrow."

"But Mom and Dad will both be there," I protested.

"We can pull it off," Pam countered. "You look good in my dress. Besides, Dad will be too embarrassed to say anything if he notices, and Mom will just follow his lead."

I had visions of Judgment Day when all our sins would be announced to the whole world.

A baptism of sins?

Pam put her hand on my arm. "It's going to be okay, Brian."

"I'm not doing this every week," I made sure to clarify.

Pam smiled and pulled out her phone. She made a call, and we waited in silence over the next several minutes for the cab to arrive. I wondered if the temple would need to be rededicated after what we'd done today. I wondered if we'd end up in the Telestial Kingdom after we died.

And then I wondered if it would be feasible for me to take my sister's place at Girls Camp this summer, if I let Judi in on the plan.

That Time the Single Adults in My Ward All Decided They Wanted to be Murdered

Over thirty years have passed since that night when I first realized I was never going to be successful at leading a Mormon life. I was the female Single Adult rep for the Metairie ward, the suburb of New Orleans where the stake center was located. Arthur was the male rep.

He'd finished a mission to London five years previously and frequently reminded us that many of the early Church leaders had served there as well. He often practiced making up profound quotes he could use in his talks at General Conference when he eventually became an apostle. Prior to my call, there used to be just one rep for each ward but the stake was trying to be more inclusive of women. Looking back, I expect it was also just to make sure at least two Singles from each ward attended the activities.

Since we were in "the mission field," we didn't have an Institute building for our Wednesday evening classes. We met with the Institute teacher in the Relief Society room of the stake center. I was twenty-one, in my senior year at the University of New Orleans studying Chemistry, and this was only the second year we had a real live CES teacher for Institute. Before, it had always just been someone's third or fourth calling, and the folks standing up before the class were usually no better prepared than most Sunday School teachers.

Meaning we were lucky if they'd even read the lesson ahead of time.

But Brother Belanger knew his stuff and made the lessons fun. One evening, we learned mnemonic devices for remembering all the presidents of the Church. Everyone knew Joseph Smith and Brigham Young, of course, so there was no need for anything special there. But what about the third prophet?

"Imagine a tricycle," Brother Belanger said. "It has three wheels, and there's this grown man riding. He looks ridiculous, and his coat gets caught in the wheels and is torn. He really needs a tailor. So John Taylor is the third president."

He went on with the others. What kind of image could we come up with for the number four? Well, a dog has four legs. And it goes "Ruff, ruff." So Wilford Woodruff was the fourth president. And so on. The thing is, as stupid as it was, we all learned the names of every single prophet up through the current one, Ezra Taft Benson, and all these years later, I can still tell you the names in order. Or out of order, for that matter. Just tell me the number and I can remember the mnemonic device for it and the associated Mormon leader.

Thank God I learned something useful at church.

That night Brother Belanger gave what I suppose was a routine lesson. I don't even recall what it was about. I just remember the conclusion. "You know," he said, "the scriptures tell us no one knows the day or the hour of Christ's return. But..." and here he waited till we were all staring at him with anticipation, "...they don't say no one knows the *year*."

We were thunderstruck with the possibilities. The leaders might actually know the exact year of Christ's return! Somehow, that made the Second Coming seem more imminent, though really, there was no reason to think the year in question wasn't 2264. But at his words, a jolt of electricity flashed through the room. I remember sensing a chill go up my spine.

And I remember feeling grateful I was capable of being touched by the Spirit. So often when it came to the gospel, I felt nothing.

After the lesson was over, the Singles drifted to the gym, where most of them started a game of volleyball. There weren't many of us, a handful from each ward. I hung out at the edge of the gym near the kitchen with a few of the other Singles from my congregation. Because of a shortage of classrooms, I'd had to meet in that kitchen with my teacher when I was a MIA Maid.

"When do you think the Second Coming will be?" Rafael asked. He'd served a mission in his native Guatemala, though his family had come to the U.S. when he was two. His family had made a concerted effort to assimilate right from the beginning, so he'd learned most of his Spanish in the MTC.

"Hopefully by the year 2000," Drew replied. He was fit and attractive, and I'd fantasized about him more than once, but he had an annoying habit of constantly complaining about mosquito bites or other minor ailments. "I don't think I can hold out much longer than that."

He batted at a fly only he could see, and we all laughed. After all, we liked him well enough despite his failings. All of us had some, and as young adults breaking away from our parents for the first time, we felt a camaraderie and loyalty to support one another.

Unless someone made the kind of mistake I was about to.

"Why don't the leaders just tell us the year?" I asked. "It would be so much easier to plan our lives if they gave us something to work with."

"We're supposed to plan our lives in faith, not in knowledge." That was Darla. She was almost thirty and would soon need to start hanging out with the back-up Singles group, the one whose members the young Singles thought of as old and creepy or old and pathetic, depending on their gender.

"But it's still faith even if the leaders tell us the year," I pointed out. "We still have to believe that they know what they're talking about, that they're not just some guys making stuff up."

"Yes, but if we're *good* Mormons, it's as if God said it himself, so it doesn't take *much* faith."

"I wish they'd tell us, too," said Xiomara. She was Rafael's sister, just eighteen but looking younger. She'd barely started attending activities. Her first name was Betty, to sound more American, but Xiomara insisted on using her middle name. "If it's only ten or fifteen years, I'll wait to have kids so they don't have to live through Armageddon, but if it's not till 2040 or something, I can get married now."

"I don't want to wait any longer than I have to to get married," said Darla, "whether Jesus is coming soon or not." She glanced down at her left hand.

I noticed that Arthur was looking at Xiomara's breasts.

"That's the thing," said Drew. "We're supposed to live our lives without knowing."

"But why?" I asked. Wasn't the whole point of having a living prophet that we didn't need to live in ignorance like the rest of the world? "*Why* is that better?"

He frowned. "It just is."

I'm sure I frowned in return. There were so many things in Mormonism we had to accept as givens, yet to me, they weren't givens at all. Why was it important for me to have six or seven children now in a world full of hate and crime, when I could wait till the Millennium to raise them in peace and happiness? Why was it so important I stay at home with the kids instead of finding a man who was happy to do that while I was the one to pursue a career?

Surely, what was important was that one person in the relationship be there for the kids. Did it have to be *me*?

And why was it okay for Bishop Moss to ask overly detailed questions about my sexuality during worthiness interviews? Surely, it was enough that I confessed to masturbation. Did he *really* need to ask if my nipples got hard when I did it?

Darla decided to change the subject, and for the next few minutes we reminisced about the canoe trip we'd gone on recently. Darla had lost her pants when her canoe capsized in some rapids on the Bogue Chitto River. I suspected she'd assisted the rushing water in its task, as she'd switched canoes right after the incident to take a seat in front of a guy from the Westbank Ward I knew she had her eye on.

Arthur had made it the entire trip without falling into the water but then capsized just as he was trying to get ashore at the end, growing quite angry when people laughed at him. At one point, even Drew insisted he wouldn't go any further, that we had to send a helicopter back to pick him up. And Rafael had cut his hand on a submerged tree coming around a sharp bend. Apparently, he'd learned some Spanish curse words on his mission.

But now everyone talked as if they'd had the grandest time of their life.

"We should all go skydiving sometime," Drew suggested.

I imagined him wishing for a helicopter halfway down to the ground.

"I don't know," said Xiomara. "Sounds dangerous."

"So what if it is?" Drew replied. "It'd be a quick death."

"Better than burning to death," said Arthur.

"Those are our choices?" I asked. "Why?"

"I want to die of a heart attack," Rafael said, "like my grandmother. It was quick."

"Not cancer, though," said Xiomara. "Like Tia Maria."

A volleyball rolled up against my right foot. I leaned down to pick it up and tossed it back to one of the players out on the basketball court.

"What about dying in a plane crash?" asked Darla. "That's pretty quick."

Drew nodded. "But those last two minutes would be pure terror. Would you really want to die right after crapping your pants?"

"The thing is," said Arthur, "all those deaths are meaningless. The best way is to die *for* something. I want to die a martyr."

"Me, too." Rafael's brows furrowed. "I kind of hoped it would happen during my mission. I didn't baptize much, and I was worried I'd never make it to the Celestial Kingdom if I didn't get a few bonus points."

"I don't see how I'll ever make it, either," Darla agreed. "I'm not married, no one even asks me on dates..." She glanced at Drew. "And sometimes, I drink tea." She looked about quickly to see how we'd take that revelation. As if we didn't already know all this about her. "I need the bonus points, too."

"And wouldn't it just be *easier* to be killed for the gospel?" asked Arthur. "Finishing grad school seems so much harder. Plus, there's all the temptation we have to face every day of our lives." He glanced at Xiomara's chest again. "Satan tries even more, you know, with the ones the Lord has foreordained to be leaders. And what's the point of having a good career, anyway? You still have to pay taxes." He shook his head. "The only thing that really matters is making it to the Celestial Kingdom, so the sooner we die, the better."

"Some martyrs get burned to death," said Xiomara.

"I already said that one's out."

"Do you get to choose how you'll be martyred?" I asked.

"I wonder if martyrs ever get injected with an instant poison?"

"I want to get shot in the head."

"How about stabbing?"

"I don't know. Even a paper cut hurts pretty bad."

I put my hand over my mouth to hide a giggle.

"How do *you* want to die, Michelle?" Drew demanded.

"I don't want to die at all," I said.

The others stared at me in astonishment. "You don't want to die a martyr?" Darla's frown looked cartoonish.

"Nope."

"You think you're good enough to make it to the Celestial Kingdom on your own?" Arthur asked, his eyes wide. He wasn't snarky, just incredulous.

I shrugged. "I trust Heavenly Father to send me where I belong. I don't think a lot about it."

Several of the others gasped. "You don't think about it?" Darla whispered.

"I'm more worried about remembering my equations for class."

And that's when I knew I'd crossed a line. A few of the others visibly stepped away from me, and every one of the others looked as if I'd just spit on the Book of Mormon. No one said anything mean or critical. In fact, no one said anything at all for the next few minutes.

I remembered the comments some of the sisters in Relief Society often made that I wasn't as focused on motherhood as I needed to be, but I'd always been able to convince them I was simply looking for a husband with an advanced degree.

The Singles had been less judgmental, though Arthur had pointed out once that Chemistry was a good major for someone who was going to need to cook the rest of her life. But what I'd just said revealed an awkward truth—I did worry about my studies more than I worried about the Church. What I'd said seemed so innocuous to me, but the others instinctively knew what it represented.

And it was unforgivable.

Finally, after such an awkward silence I considered excusing myself to the bathroom, Arthur spoke up. "We have a Singles dance the weekend after this one," he said. "I sure hope I can find someone there to take on the temple trip."

Darla looked down at her feet, probably contemplating how she wouldn't be able to pass any questions about the Word of Wisdom in the temple recommend interview. I wanted to tell her to lie.

"Ooh, I love dances!" said Xiomara. "I hope lots of returned missionaries show up." All the girls knew these dances were the only Single Adult activities the out-ot-town Mormon students at Tulane Medical School ever attended.

I listened to the others gush for the next few minutes, but for some reason, their enthusiasm made me feel the way my brother must have felt when he received his mission call to Nebraska, after he'd studied German for two years hoping for a foreign mission. I enjoyed dances, too, and I did want to share my life with a soulmate, if there were such a thing, but for the first time, I realized I was never going to meet the man of my dreams at a Singles dance.

It would probably be better if I just stayed home that night and studied. A couple of my classmates had already asked if we could be study partners, and I'd always put them off because I didn't feel comfortable making friends with non-members. Perhaps now might be a good time to revisit that question.

I looked out onto the basketball court and watched for a moment as the other Singles lobbed the volleyball back and forth to each other. Then I excused myself and walked out to my car.

I never attended another Singles activity the rest of the time I was still a Mormon.

As it turned out, of course, I didn't meet the man of my dreams until after I'd earned my PhD. Alex was the nanny I hired to watch my baby while I taught my first classes at Chapel Hill. He was a secular Jew and taught Crystal to read by the time she was four. He did take me to the temple a few times—Temple Sinai.

Though we never married, he couldn't be a truer father to our daughter if we had. He even published a book about parenting, asking for Crystal's permission to include some of the more embarrassing anecdotes. He studied enough chemistry that he and I could carry on intelligent conversations at home. He was there for me during my bout with cancer, and I've supported him in his run for the city council.

And during those monthly family dinners when Crystal and her girlfriend come to visit, we all sit around the table and talk with excitement about how we want to live.

The Translation of Elder Bauman

"Let's go kayaking," Elder Bauman said as soon as we got off our knees Wednesday morning.

I was shocked by the suggestion. What was he thinking? "The Devil has power over the water," I replied.

"We won't be in the water," my companion pointed out. "We'll be in kayaks."

I shook my head. "No, Elder. Let's do something else for P-Day."

Elder Bauman sat on the edge of his bed and rubbed his chin. I thought about saying something gentle to guide him. We weren't allowed to sit on our beds during the day. We might fall asleep and be unproductive. I'd already had to report my senior companion to the zone leaders once for such an infraction. But given that today was Preparation Day, I decided to let it pass.

"We rode the Ferris wheel down on the Seattle waterfront last week," Elder Bauman mused. "And we watched the boats going through the locks the week before."

"Both activities which brought us in contact with water," I reminded him. We'd suffered the consequences both times. The following day after each event, an investigator we were teaching had gotten upset with me for absolutely no reason and turned away from the gospel. "Why don't we go to a museum?"

Elder Bauman frowned. "How about going on a hike?" he countered. "I hear Mt. Si is an easy one."

I was shocked again by the suggestion. We were expressly forbidden from doing anything that put our lives at risk. People got lost and died while hiking all the time. "That sounds dangerous," I said.

"A thousand people hike that trail every week, Elder Randolph."

"Where did you get those figures?" He hadn't been sneaking time on the Internet again, had he?

"From Brother Torgeson." Elder Bauman's jaw tightened. "And don't you curl your lip at me."

We continued to discuss what to do for the day's outing over the next several minutes. It turned out my companion had already gotten information from Brother Torgeson on which bus to catch from which corner to get us out to North Bend, so I finally assented. It might give us something to talk to Brother Torgeson about next time we stopped by his place while trying to reactivate him.

We put on our jeans and P-Day shirts, grabbed our jackets, plastic gloves, and a plastic garbage bag each, and headed downtown. Elder Bauman wasn't happy that my compromise required us to pick up trash for half an hour before catching the bus, but he knew my philosophy— Righteousness Before Fun.

"This is Right Below Fantasizing," he muttered as we walked along scooping up discarded McDonalds cups and empty cigarette packs.

I wasn't sure exactly what he meant by that, but I knew he was sinning to say it. I almost insisted we turn back home. But to be honest, I kind of wanted to get out in the wilderness for a while, too. I was from Chicago, where the lake was about the only bit of Nature close enough to visit.

From our apartment on Capitol Hill, Elder Bauman and I could see the Olympics in one direction and the Cascades in the other. I'd forbidden a trip to Snoqualmie Falls once a few months ago because of the water issue, and I'd always regretted it. Not enough to suggest we go there on another P-Day, but enough that I hadn't fought very hard today against heading to North Bend.

I wasn't sure why I even felt the need to fight at all. I suppose it was simply that if Elder Bauman was making the suggestion, there had to be something wrong with it. He'd sat on a bench in Cal Anderson Park for two hours one afternoon last week, refusing to talk to people about the Church, while he listened to music on his earbuds.

He said he was listening to the Mormon Tabernacle Choir, but he also refused to let me verify. Another day, he'd spent over an hour—an hour!—in the conservatory in Volunteer Park looking at the flowers. An hour we should have been working for the Lord.

Who wouldn't be suspicious of anything Elder Bauman said?

"Kind of makes you want to go to Starbucks, doesn't it?" Elder Bauman asked, sniffing an empty coffee cup.

"Don't be disgusting."

He was never going to make it to the end of his mission. I still had sixteen months to go, but the mission president had already told me if I kept up my good attitude, I'd be senior on the next transfers and a district leader soon after that.

I couldn't wait to be higher than Elder Bauman. Even if he was no longer my companion by that point, I could still show him the way to be a good missionary. It was as important to strengthen weak members as it was to baptize new converts. That's why we kept stopping at Brother Torgeson's house.

Before long, we were on the 208 heading east, Elder Bauman looking out the window, nodding his head to the music coming from his phone. I thought about talking to one of the other passengers about the Church but decided that since it was P-Day, the Lord wouldn't mind if I closed my eyes for a few minutes.

Suffice it to say that the trail entrance was not an easy walk from the bus stop in North Bend, but we eventually made it to the starting point. "Want to race up the mountain?" Elder Bauman asked with a grin.

"We might get separated."

Elder Bauman smiled. But he knew that being apart was one of the biggest sins in the mission field. "We could go up on different paths," he suggested. "You can take the trail and I can go through the forest."

"Why don't we join that couple over there?" I returned. "We could tell them we're missionaries." I didn't want to do that any more than he did, but I knew I needed to make such a suggestion to end up at the compromise I wanted.

We walked up the trail together without any other company. Elder Bauman kept asking me to listen to the bird calls. I quizzed Elder Bauman on his scripture verses.

"I'm the senior companion," he said. "I'm supposed to be guiding you."

"Feel free," I said.

Elder Bauman stopped, put his hand on the trunk of a fir tree, and wiped his brow. "Elder Randolph," he said, "you may well end up a General Authority one day if you don't change your behavior…" I smiled. "…but you'll be the one everybody hates. You've got to lighten up."

We didn't talk for the next twenty minutes. My mother had told me something similar my last year in Seminary. My bishop had told me almost the same thing in my interview before sending off my mission papers. Even my stake president had pulled me aside after setting me apart and then given me a warning.

"Don't be a dick," he said.

I suspected these people were all just spiritual peasants. People who didn't have what it took to rise to greatness. The mission president here thought I was wonderful. He was much more in tune with the Spirit than my bishop had ever been.

When Elder Bauman and I made it to the top, we stood and stared at the incredible vista for several minutes while we rested. A few other hikers milled about, oohing and aahing as well. The Celestial Kingdom would be so much better than this, I wanted to tell them. It was *important* to be a good Mormon.

"Don't do it," Elder Bauman warned.

"Do what?"

"I see that look in your eyes."

"It's called the Spirit."

"Try living without the Spirit for a while."

My mouth fell open at such heresy. Elder Bauman's eyes narrowed, his jaw tightened, and he pointed to the trail back down. "I'm walking back without you," he said. "If you try to catch up to me, I swear I'll punch your face out." With that, he took off down the trail.

I was going to have to report him.

I waited a few minutes and then began strolling casually back down the mountain. I could use this opportunity to really commune with Heavenly Father. The going was much easier in this direction, obviously, and I felt relaxed for the first time in ages.

I found myself pausing to look at the view through the trees when possible, pausing to caress the needles on the nearby trees, pausing to smell the earthiness of the area. I felt light and free and wondered if Elder Bauman's negativity had been keeping me down. Perhaps I should request an emergency transfer.

I remembered something my father had told me. "Don't put on a show."

But my righteousness wasn't a show. I really was righteous. It wasn't prideful to say so. And yet as I continued on the path downward, I began to wonder if I should apologize to my companion. Or at least buy him a hot chocolate. I wouldn't say anything about giving in, but he'd know that my going into a coffee shop at all was a major concession.

I could be humble as well as righteous.

My plans evaporated, though, as soon as I reached the bottom of the mountain. Elder Bauman was nowhere to be found. Had he strayed off the trail? Had he joined up with another hiker and shared a beer? Had he gone back to the bus stop and headed home without me?

I tried to call his cell phone but there was no reception. I realized again how irresponsible the man could be, and how much he needed my guidance.

There'd be no hot chocolate tonight.

I waited for an hour. Then two. Finally, I walked back to the bus stop alone and caught the bus back to Seattle. I was fuming by the time I reached our apartment. But my companion wasn't there, either. I was so mad I slapped the kitchen table. When Elder Bauman still hadn't arrived by 5:00, the time P-Day officially ended and we had to start proselytizing again, I called the zone leaders.

"I'm going to have to tell the mission president you didn't stay with your companion," Elder Crenshaw said curtly.

The zone leaders called the president, who called the police, but it was too late in the day to start a search party. Rescuers combed Mt. Si the following day but couldn't find even a trace of Elder Bauman. The mission president phoned his parents. Elder Bauman hadn't called home to say he was leaving the mission. The police tried tracking him down through his debit card, but there had been no transactions. There were no pings from his cell phone.

I never saw Elder Bauman again. But four months later at a zone conference, while I was still getting used to yet another senior companion, the mission president made an announcement.

"I'm sure you're all still wondering about Elder Bauman," he said. "I'm sure you're all concerned about him. But after much prayer and fasting, it has been revealed to me that Elder Bauman was translated. He is no longer on this Earth."

There was a gasp from the missionaries in attendance. This had only happened once before that we knew about. A missionary in another country had been driving a van full of missionaries and had been swept away crossing a creek, or by a flood, or something.

I couldn't remember the exact details. I just remembered it had something to do with the Devil and the Devil's power over water. All the missionaries had been saved, except the driver, whose body was never found. His mission president finally declared that the missing elder had been translated.

And I'd been in the presence of greatness myself and not realized it.

It was almost like walking with a beggar and not recognizing it was Jesus. I pinched my arm hard to punish myself.

I wondered if Elder Bauman being with me had been the influence he needed to attain the level of righteousness that allowed him to be translated.

But he'd been the one translated, not me. Maybe there was something I could have learned from him.

I frowned.

Maybe I wasn't as humble as I thought.

I really did want to be good.

The rest of the zone conference went as usual, concluding with all of us bearing our testimonies. Then Elder Croft and I started back for our apartment. "I'm exhausted," he said. "How about we call it a day and don't work tonight?"

I opened my mouth to protest and then stopped. "All right, Elder," I agreed with a sigh. I thought about the MP3 player I'd confiscated months ago from Bauman and kept in my suitcase. "Why don't we listen to some music instead?"

Casting the Last Stone

Relief Society was letting out and Marlene started gathering her things. She was moving slowly, a lot on her mind. She'd only recently been baptized into the Mormon Church and still found some of its concepts confusing. But it had changed her life for the better, and she was going to learn everything she had to know.

Just as she started for the door, April and Frances, who'd been sitting on either side of her during the lesson, blocked her path. "Marlene," April said, "you've got to help us."

"Yes, Marlene," Frances agreed, "please."

"What is it?" asked Marlene. She wasn't up to teaching one of the Relief Society classes just yet. And if it was a regular calling they were talking about, wasn't the bishop the one who was supposed to ask? She wasn't sure she fully understood how everything worked at this point, so she looked at the women in anticipation.

April and Frances glanced at each other nervously. Then Frances looked over her shoulder while April leaned forward. "We need sex tips," April whispered. "Our husbands aren't happy with us, and we're afraid they'll start looking at porn and…and…who knows what, if we don't start doing a better job."

Marlene's mouth fell open. Both these women were in their mid-forties, over ten years her senior. "And what makes you think I can help?" she asked. "I've never been married, you know."

"Yes, but…but…"

Marlene raised an eyebrow.

"You're so young and blond and…buxom," April said.

"Uh-huh."

"And people have been saying things," said Frances.

So there it was. The only people she'd told about her years as a prostitute were the sister missionaries who'd taught her, their zone leaders who interviewed her for baptism, and Bishop Greggson. She hadn't told a single member other than that. She distinctly remembered one of the sister missionaries teaching her that gossip was a sin.

So who had blabbed?

"I don't feel comfortable discussing this," Marlene said carefully. April and Frances looked at each other nervously again. "Perhaps you could talk to a professional sex therapist." She shrugged helplessly. "Or buy a book at the bookstore. I'm sure there are some videos—"

"Oh, my Lord!" breathed Frances.

"Oh, heavens!" said April.

Marlene set her books down and took both women by the hand. "I appreciate you trying to make me feel wanted, but I really don't want this information getting around. I'm trying to start a new life in the gospel." She leaned forward and gave both women pecks on the cheek. Then she picked up her books again and walked out of the room.

She had another fifteen minutes to wait before her appointment with the bishop. She spent most of the time fretting over whether he was the leaker.

The term brought back an unpleasant memory from the past. She thrust it out of her mind.

"Sister Meadows," Bishop Greggson said a few minutes later, "so nice to see you. Come into my office." He was almost fifty, with graying temples and smile lines on his forehead and around his mouth. Marlene entered and sat in the chair in front of his desk. "What can I do for you today?"

Marlene leaned forward and put both hands flat on the bishop's desk. "It's like this," she said. "I'm not going to be able to pay my tithing this month."

Bishop Greggson frowned. "Oh, dear," he said. "That's a problem."

"Bishop, I don't need to tell you I make a lot less at Wal-Mart than I made at my last job." She wondered if she should confront him about the leak. "I can just barely pay my rent as it is. If I pay tithing, I'll get evicted."

Bishop Greggson leaned back as if to put some distance between them. He pressed his palms together and tapped the tips of his fingers against each other. "The thing is," he said, "the Lord can't bless you if you don't obey the commandments. What you need to do is pay your tithing, and then the Church can offer you assistance until you become self-sufficient."

"I'm self-sufficient *now*," Marlene returned. "I just can't afford to support you, too."

Bishop Greggson chuckled. "I'll stop by your apartment Tuesday evening and pick up your check." He gave her a wink. "And then I'll set you up with the Bishop's Storehouse so you can get some food."

"But Bishop—"

"You've made some big changes in your life, Marlene. There's no sense going only 90% of the way. You need to embrace this 100% to make it to the Celestial Kingdom."

He was almost certainly right. Marlene had been reluctant to get into sex work, but once she committed herself, she'd done well. The same principle surely applied.

She bit her lip. "Can I ask you something first?"

"What's that?"

"Did you tell anyone about my past?"

Bishop Greggson frowned for a moment but then smiled again, scooting his chair back another inch. "I did tell a few select sisters," he said. "I thought they'd be more understanding and helpful if they knew the whole story."

"I see."

"I only spoke to those I felt directed to tell by the Spirit."

Marlene looked at the filing cabinet in the corner of the room. She looked at the window behind the bishop with its shade pulled down so no one could see who was in his office. She looked at the portrait of the First Presidency on the wall. Then she nodded.

"All right. I'll have the check ready by Tuesday."

The bishop showed up at her apartment as scheduled, and Marlene handed the check over to him. When he asked if she needed anything in return, she said, "Can you get me some help moving this Saturday?"

"You're moving?"

"I think I need a studio apartment for a while. I can't afford this one bedroom any longer. And the new place is on a better bus route."

Bishop Greggson smiled. "That sounds like a good idea. We'll be able to give you less money."

"But Bishop—"

"I'll have the Elders Quorum here first thing Saturday morning. You'll still be within ward boundaries?"

Marlene nodded. She'd thought about moving closer to work, but there was no point in having her infamy spread any farther than necessary. She had to deal with it now. She was a damaged woman and that was all there was to it. No use in hiding. Her Visiting Teachers had stopped by Sunday afternoon and, as nice as they were, gently pointed out that Marlene needed new clothing for church or people would start to talk.

Start, she thought.

Her shifts the rest of the week at Wal-Mart were tedious, ringing up customers one after another after another. She recognized one of them, a chubby man with an unattractive hint of hair on his chin, but he didn't seem to recognize her. That was a relief, anyway.

Marlene felt just the slightest temptation to remind him about their last encounter and ask if he wanted to see her again, but she knew she'd never be able to look herself in the mirror if she fell away from the Church so soon after discovering it. She put his groceries in a bag and the bag back in his cart.

She looked after him as he walked away.

Friday night after she returned home, Marlene packed up the few things she could arrange to take with her. She'd snagged a few boxes from the back of the store and so made quick work of it. She gave everything she couldn't take to Jonah and Geraldine next door, who'd bailed her out of jail a few times.

As she knelt down beside her bed that night, she prayed. "Heavenly Father, help this be a new start for me." She squeezed her eyes shut so tightly they hurt. "Help me be the person you want me to be."

There'd never been anyone she wanted to please before. Other than sexually, of course. It was invigorating to have someone to make proud now.

Marlene was waiting by the door when the elders showed up Saturday morning, most of them in their early thirties, though Tyler looked almost forty. Jason, a muscular young carpenter, had brought his pickup truck, and Seth, with the kind of Dad body she knew too well, had brought his SUV. Some of the other elders just came with empty car trunks and empty back seats.

But that was all she needed. Within half an hour, the smaller vehicles were packed. All that was left was to load the bed frame and mattresses onto the pickup next to the love seat. Jason and Tyler worked together while the others headed to the new apartment with Marlene's key.

Marlene stayed behind with the remaining two elders so she could lock the door when they were finished and bring that key to the apartment manager's office. She sure hoped she could get her deposit back.

"Hey, Marlene," Tyler said, tightening a strap around the furniture, "you up for a housewarming party tonight?"

"Oh, that's very sweet of you," said Marlene. "But there's no need."

"Not that." He laughed. "I mean…well, you know…"

Marlene looked directly at the man. He hadn't shaved this morning, and his nose hairs needed trimming. His shirt was too tight, suggesting he was unnaturally proud of his body despite being ten pounds overweight. He scratched casually at his crotch. She knew exactly the kind of guy she was dealing with. "No, I don't know."

Tyler grinned and whispered. "Once a whore, always a whore, right?"

Marlene kept her face blank. It seemed everyone in the ward knew about her past.

"What do you charge?" Tyler asked, making sure Jason was still inside the apartment and couldn't overhear. "A hundred dollars? It'll help pay your rent, won't it?"

Marlene wanted to scratch his face, the way she'd done to that police officer who offered not to arrest her last year if she'd give him a freebie. But that hadn't gone particularly well, and she knew this probably wouldn't, either.

"I'm a Latter-day Saint," she replied calmly. "And I'll lose my Church welfare if I'm not worthy."

"No one has to know."

"I'll know."

Jason was coming down from the apartment with the last sofa cushion, so Tyler grabbed Marlene's arm and hissed. "I can tell the bishop you solicited me and you won't get any help at all anymore."

Marlene looked toward Jason, who seemed to be approaching so, so slowly. But when he looked in their direction, she thought she could see a gleam in his eye. He might not be the help she wanted.

"Okay," she said. "You have my new address. Help me get everything settled in the new place, and you can come back over later tonight. 8:00."

Tyler grinned. "I think this is the beginning of a wonderful friendship."

Two hours later, the few pieces of furniture were situated where Marlene wanted them. Her kitchen items were in the cabinets. Her clothes were in the closet. Even her television was hooked up. Her one painting, a Monet print, hung over the love seat.

She frowned as she surveyed her surroundings. Everything looked so tiny and cramped in the new place. But the important thing was that she had her scriptures. Marlene read all the way through Alma. It took a while because her mind kept wandering and she had to reread the last few verses over again, time after time.

What if Bishop Greggson could sense her sins the next time they met? She wondered if it would really be so bad to have sex just a few times a month. She did like sex, after all. Most of the time. And she could even pay tithing on the extra money she made. The bishop would like that.

But if her past had gotten around the ward this quickly, what would happen with the news of her present? She wanted the sisters in the ward to like her. Perhaps she should call April and Frances and talk to them, after all.

When she finished the last chapter of Alma, Marlene realized she didn't feel any better now than she had before she started. She heated some Ramen noodles, prayed one last time, and made up her mind while spooning down the unsatisfying mixture. She made the preparations she needed to make, took a shower, and sat on the love seat waiting for Tyler's arrival.

At 7:55, there was a knock at the door. Marlene ushered Tyler into the studio, watching his eyes light up when he saw the bed with the covers already pulled down. "Looks like you're as hot to tangle as I am," he said with a grin.

"Well, I usually like to talk to my clients a few minutes before we get started. It makes the sex more fun for both of us."

"Whatever," said Tyler. "You want me to talk about my dick?"

Marlene laughed. "I want you to tell me exactly what it is about your sex life with your wife that's lacking."

Tyler frowned, thought for a moment, and then nodded. "All right. The biggest problem is that all she does is lie there. She won't make any noise, won't go down on me, won't let me do anything fun."

"What makes you think I'll be fun?"

Tyler grinned again and reached for Marlene's breasts. "No one with knockers like these can be boring," he said.

Marlene forced a modest smile. "So you really want me to lie to the bishop and have you over here on a regular basis?"

"We *all* lie to the bishop," said Tyler. "You certainly don't think this is the first time I've hired a hooker."

Marlene nodded. "I guess not. And I suppose that's good news."

"Why's that?"

"It means you're experienced. Experienced men are always more fun."

Tyler licked his lips. "Then why don't we both get some more experience right now?"

Marlene stood and motioned to the bed. "You get undressed and climb in. I'll just run into the bathroom for one last rinse with mouthwash."

Tyler's shirt was off before she reached the bathroom. She went in and closed the door behind her, giving the man another moment to finish disrobing. Then she opened the bathroom door again.

"What the fuck!" Tyler shouted, pulling the sheet up to his chin.

"Tyler," Marlene said, "I thought it best if our relationship had some kind of ecclesiastical approval." She pointed to the man beside her. "So I asked Bishop Greggson to come over tonight, too." She smiled and patted the bishop on the shoulder.

He looked decidedly uncomfortable. But he looked angry even more than uncomfortable. "Did you hear everything okay?" she asked.

"I heard every word," he replied. "Tyler, get your damn clothes back on."

As Tyler fumbled about for his garments, Marlene turned back toward the bishop. "And now, Bishop Greggson, I'd like to discuss my welfare check again." She adjusted Bishop Greggson's tie. "I want three hundred dollars more each month than we agreed on earlier."

"What?"

She leaned close and whispered in his ear. "Or I'll have Tyler here tell everyone he saw you in my apartment after hours. I'm sure I could make some kind of arrangement with him."

Bishop Greggson nodded weakly, Tyler finished dressing, and soon both men scurried out of the apartment. Marlene poured herself a glass of 7-Up, sat down on the love seat, and began reading the Book of Helaman.

Secret Agent of the Esplanade Ward

Katrina said goodbye to her "friends" as the Single Adult Family Home Evening came to a close. She was always cordial and polite when hanging out with the Mormons, pretending to be one of them. The life of a religious spinster had been her cover for years now.

But as soon as she got back home to her apartment near the St. Louis cemetery at the end of Esplanade Avenue, she poured herself a glass of vodka. A good spy had to keep up her drinking skills if she didn't want to be compromised on a future mission.

Katrina squeezed her eyes shut and shook her head as the fiery liquid went down. Her first taste of alcohol had been during her days as a missionary in London. That was where she'd originally been recruited as an agent. She'd been clumsy back then, of course. No experience. And it got her sent home.

Worse than the shame of leaving her mission early, though, was the horror of watching her mother confined to a hospital bed days later, incubated because she could no longer breathe on her own, poisoned by the Russians in retaliation for Katrina's attempt at filtration.

Her beloved mother had succumbed after two long weeks of complete misery. The devastation forced Katrina to return to the CIA, demanding further training and another mission. She needed to have meaning in her life. She needed to avenge her mother's murder.

Katrina enrolled at the University of New Orleans and took every Russian course available. Her superiors insisted on as little contact as possible, so she had to do everything as if she weren't connected to them. Learning that Syllabic alphabet had been hard, though. She kept earning C's and D's, retaking the courses over and over.

Eventually, though, she was given another official assignment. She was to make contact with a Russian she met at the Greek Orthodox church on Robert E. Lee. Since there was no Russian embassy or consummate in New Orleans, Russians had to make their contacts under Greek cover. She'd slipped a piece of paper in the man's coat during services and made her way out without being seen.

She'd succeeded. So she was given a second mission. And a third.

That was all years ago.

Katrina drank another glass of vodka, and then one more. But Popov was expensive, and she lived on a very small stipend disguised as a Disability payment. Not that she didn't really deserve Disability. You couldn't work as a spy for long without recurring *some* injuries.

She shuddered as she remembered the incident with the streetcar, but she'd had no choice other than to jump off.

After three glasses of vodka, Katrina slept soundly, though with a butcher knife beneath her pillow, as usual. She hoped she wouldn't have to use it again.

Tuesday was a new day, and Katrina headed for the Audubon Zoo uptown. She bought a small bag of popcorn and meandered through the exhibits. The monkeys were always disgusting, the birds thrilling, the caged elephants so sad, no artificial compound large enough to accommodate their needs. The alligator pond reminded her of a narrow escape in Jean Lafitte Park. Another CIA agent working with her that day hadn't been so lucky. But Katrina was smart. She could learn even from others' mistakes.

Aaah, thought Katrina, coming to a stop in front of the exhibit where she was to make her contact. She loved the kimono dragons. Beautiful yet fierce. Just like she was. She finished her bag of popcorn and tried to look about casually so as not to draw suspicion.

Where was her contact? She glanced at her watch, wondering if something had happened to him, if her mission was compromised, if she might be in danger. A tall, muscular man with an angular jaw moved closer, and she tensed in case she had to flee.

But the guy moved on and Katrina relaxed. Thirty-five minutes later—thirty-five!—another lone man stopped near her, slurping flavored ice. He was pudgy, almost as overweight as she was, and not very attractive. The perfect cover for the CIA. When the man glanced in her direction, she smiled. He did a double take, way too obvious for a seasoned agent, and she smiled again. She'd have to teach him how to be more subtle.

They were soon back in his safe house, where Katrina performed the necessary sexual favors that had been part of her job for years. Funny how her cover was to be part of a religion that condemned such behavior, and yet in order to fully serve God and country, she willingly developed her seduction skills. After they finished and she began putting her clothes back on, she discreetly set a memory stick she'd picked up at a coffeehouse on the bedside table.

"What's this?" the man asked, laughing. "Nude pics?"

Not bad, thought Katrina. He knew the place might be bugged. She just smiled sweetly, buttoned her last button, and walked out the door.

She went directly from the other agent's apartment to the public library on St. Charles, where she checked out a DVD of *The Notebook*. Every time her superiors needed to give her a new assignment, they did it through this movie. She slipped the DVD into her player at home and watched the story unfold. It was a bit annoying that the message never came until near the end of the film, but it was a good film, so she put up with it.

Only her personal DVD player had the capacity to decode the message, so if anyone else saw the movie by mistake, it would look just like a normal version of the film to them. But in Katrina's tailored version, near the end of the story when the characters kiss in the nursing home, James Garner said, "MoMA. Wednesday. 2:00 p.m." And that was the end of the message.

Katrina had made lots of contacts at the Museum of Modern Art. She liked those assignments because City Park was walking distance from her apartment and she didn't have to catch the bus. The next day in the Fabulous room, Katrina studied each Russian egg for five minutes, egg after egg after egg, waiting for the signal. Finally, a woman bumped into her next to a Fabulous clock, and Katrina headed for the bathroom, where she attached a small, round refrigerator magnet to the stall door.

It was frustrating never knowing the full details of any of her missions, but she appreciated being part of a complex operation. Everyone at church always treated her like she was a nobody. But one day, people would understand her dedication and sacrifice. Katrina kept a meticulous journal—dangerous, she knew—but she hid it carefully, and upon her death, the account of her adventures would be preserved in the Brigham Young University library so the whole world could see that a woman was perfectly capable of success in life even without having babies.

Katrina remembered the time the Russians had poisoned her after one successful assignment. She'd survived, but she'd had to undergo a hisdirectome in order to do so. Disappointing, but it wasn't as if agents could ever bother with raising children in the first place. Real life wasn't like *True Lies*.

After her part in today's drop was complete, Katrina decided to take a stroll through the park. She needed some time off after working so hard the past couple of days. She stopped near the spot where one of the Dueling Oaks used to stand, shaking her head. The city had lost so many of its great oak trees because of the saltwater flooding from Hurricane Katrina.

She shivered. The Russians had really gone overboard with that particular assassination attempt. Her superiors hadn't believed her, but why name the storm after her if they weren't trying to get her?

But she was still here, still a successful agent at the age of fifty. She started walking again, but not twenty steps later, she saw a black man at least ten years her senior, sitting on a bench. The way he looked at her was enough. Katrina had developed quite the radar for spotting other agents in the field. She sat down next to him, smiling pleasantly.

Katrina didn't really enjoy these Ethipopian contacts, always feeling a bit dirty after those unpleasant sexual favors had been performed, but she was a real citizen, willing to serve her country under any circumstances.

Thursday morning, the Visiting Teachers stopped by the apartment. "How are you feeling today, Sister Covin?"

Katrina knew her Russian ancestry was the reason she'd been recruited in the first place. It had led to an attempt several years back to make her a double agent, but she was too patriotic for such a thing.

She ushered the two middle-aged women into her home. "I'm fine," she said. "And you, Sister Sorenson?"

The Visiting Teachers sat on the stained sofa while Katrina dragged a folding chair from the kitchen into the living room for herself. They chatted about the Visiting Teaching message posted in the latest issue of the *Ensign*. Then there was more discussion about the need for Katrina to complete her own Visiting Teaching assignment. As if secret agents had time for nonsense like that.

"Are you taking your meds?" Sister Sorenson asked when the meeting drew to a close.

She meant the poison prescribed by that thoroughly incompetent doctor who was paid by the Russians. Katrina kept her smile in place. "Of course," she said.

"Because you have that gleam in your eye like you had the last time you suffered an episode."

Katrina laughed, a sound like tinkling bells. "Oh, I'm fine," she said. "Just fine. But the medication does make me sleepy, so I'm going to have to ask you to leave now so I can get in a nap."

"Oh, certainly. Certainly." The two women glanced at each other before they stood, and Katrina ushered them out the door with a smile.

"I'll be by on Sunday morning to pick you up for church," said Sister Sorenson as the door closed.

Such busybodies, thought Katrina. Sometimes, she wondered if they weren't working for the enemy, too. Always harping on the meds. If Mormons could be divided into houses like the kids at Hogwarts, Sister Sorenson would be one of the Smithereens, just like Draco. Sister Bartlett, though, she wasn't bad. She'd probably just be a Hufflebaff.

Katrina went to the bathroom to urinate. Someday, she thought, there'd be movies made about her. Maybe even a whole series. She smiled, deeply grateful to have been recruited all those years ago. It was nothing short of wonderful to have real purpose in one's life. Her mother would be proud. She couldn't wait until Judgment Day when the whole world would finally understand her value.

Katrina grabbed a washcloth to freshen up "down there" before heading out to make her next contact.

The Media Fast

"Brothers and Sisters," said Bishop Farnsworth at the close of Sacrament meeting, "our stake president has asked us to make extra special preparations for our ward conference next week. We are going to fine tune our spiritual sensitivity with a special exercise."

Sally turned to give me a frown, but I knew how important it was to support the priesthood, so I gave a little smile in return. As a member of the bishopric, I'd known this announcement was coming. It was why I'd chosen to sit with my family today rather than take my usual seat on the stand.

Like most Sundays, Terry and Leslie seemed oblivious to any information coming over the pulpit. Terry was "reading the scriptures" on his phone and Leslie had her head bowed in prayer.

The fact that her head kept slowly sinking and then jerking back up every ten or fifteen seconds told me all I needed to know about how her communication with Heavenly Father was going. But they were teenagers, and it was important to give teenagers some slack to keep them from rebelling. At least, that was what Sally kept telling me.

"President Guthrie has requested that every member of the ward hold a complete media fast for the next seven days. No TV, no radio, no Internet, no magazines, no books, no cell phones, no computer games—nothing to distract us from our spiritual link with the Lord."

Terry's head popped up and he stared at the podium in horror. Leslie was still sleeping. Sally grasped my hand and squeezed, digging her nails into my palm.

"We can, of course, do what we have to in the workplace, but at home or away, we should only read the scriptures, Church magazines, or Church books. It's just for one week out of the entire year. It'll put us in tune with the Spirit so we can fully benefit from conference next weekend. I know that President Guthrie receives revelation and inspiration for this stake, and I fully support him as our local authority."

We sang the closing hymn, listened to Brother Davis give the closing prayer, and then church was out for the day. Leslie rubbed her eyes and yawned. Terry stood up and looked directly at me. "No computer games?" he asked. "That's not fair. I need to practice every day if I'm going to be able to compete in the tournament."

I thought it ridiculous for kids to waste every waking moment on games, but Terry had in fact won $500 a few months ago. He'd wanted to buy more games with the winnings, but after I had him pay his tithing, we put 75% of what was left in his mission fund. He had another tournament coming up in a month. Sally had encouraged me to ease up on him. As long as he kept up his grades in high school, I agreed to let him compete.

"The bishop said it was okay to use the computer if it was for work," Sally said, talking to Terry, not me. "For you, computer games are work, so it's okay."

"Is it, Dad?" asked Terry.

"Is it, Kent?" Sally echoed with a raised eyebrow.

I wasn't going to contradict my wife in public, though I wished she'd waited until we'd discussed it privately. This might have been the only opportunity to get our son to do more meaningful things with his life, at least for a few days. I'd wanted him to finally start learning how to fill out Family Group sheets.

"What are you guys talking about?" Leslie asked, yawning again.

Back at the house, Sally heated some lasagna from the night before. She rarely did any heavy cooking on the Sabbath but we did like to have a special meal when we could. Sometimes, if Sally was too busy on Saturday, we might have sandwiches or canned soup for lunch on Sunday. She insisted that she deserved a day of rest like I did.

Of course, I was often in meetings from 7:00 until our three-hour block started at 11:00.

Sunday afternoon and evening went as usual. It was already a rule in our home that there be no television on the Sabbath. Sally usually read aloud from a book by one of the apostles, while the rest of us listened as a family. Things didn't get tricky until Monday morning as I was getting ready for work. "What's the weather supposed to be like today?" I asked, scarfing down some toast.

"Beats me," Sally replied. "I think this media fast is nonsense. Even regular fasting is archaic. It's like self-flagellation or walking on your knees or wearing hairshirts."

"But you won't watch any TV today while I'm gone, will you?"

Sally gave a tight smile. "You're the head of the family."

I gave her a kiss on the cheek.

Before I left, I grabbed an umbrella just in case. It was springtime in Dallas and one never knew what to expect. I kept reaching for the radio while driving and then putting my hand back on the steering wheel. After arriving at work early, I logged onto my computer. The first thing I usually did was go to my personal email and catch up on correspondence, but I realized I couldn't do that today.

It was just as well, I supposed. My boss frowned on it anyway, even if I wasn't on the clock. But there were always lulls periodically throughout the day, and I found myself frustrated I couldn't check Yahoo news or Fox or YouTube or the TV listings or the weather or…anything.

So I concentrated more on work. That's what I should have been doing anyway, I realized. Especially if I wanted to keep moving up the ladder, which would help me as a provider while also making it easier for the Lord to call me to higher positions in the Church. The stake president was inspired. That was clear.

Still, it was annoying not to be able to text Sally about what I wanted for dinner. Or to text the kids to make sure their classes were going okay. I had to let everyone keep their cell phones just in case of an emergency. I expected, though, that neither Terry nor Leslie minded getting a break from Dad. I smiled at the thought. Maybe even they'd start to see the wisdom in the stake president's request.

Soon the family was seated together around the kitchen table for dinner. "How was your day, dear?" I asked after Sally offered the blessing on the food.

"You'll soon find out," she said. "I usually go online to look up recipes, but tonight's dinner is from memory."

We were having some kind of Mediterranean dish, but most of those tasted the same to me anyway, so I took a bite and complimented Sally on the meal. Leslie picked at the food. Terry gulped it down, but then, there was little he didn't like.

It was odd not having the news on in the background.

Since Monday was always set apart for Family Home Evening, when cell phones were regularly turned off along with the television, we didn't feel any more deprived than usual. Sally taught a lesson on how cleanliness was next to godliness and went over again how the kids could do better with keeping their rooms tidy. I thought it interesting that Sally was so lenient when it came to issues which mattered to me yet more demanding when it came to issues which mattered to her.

I wasn't sure the kids cared about either set of issues. Leslie smiled vacantly and seemed to be immersed in a world of her own, staring at the paintings on the wall. Terry kept looking at his watch. I wondered if timepieces were considered media.

"It's been a long day," Sally said as we climbed into bed later. "Do you suppose it would be okay if I put Kitaro on?"

"Kitaro's not MoTab," I replied.

Sally frowned and turned out the light, and I closed my eyes. I didn't feel any more deeply in tune with the Spirit yet, but it was only the first day of the fast.

Tuesday proved to be more difficult. Even if I wasn't watching the news myself or following it online, my coworkers brought things up around the water cooler or on breaks. "Did you hear about that Mormon polygamist who was arrested in Nevada?" Gina asked.

"If he was a polygamist, he wasn't Mormon," I tried to clarify. "He was a fundamentalist." In my experience, these conversations never went well, so I tried to bow out. But the onslaught of news continued.

"What did you think about the way the cops pulled that guy off the United flight because the crew wanted his seat?" Benson asked.

"What did you think about the elementary school shooting in San Bernardino?" asked Stephanie.

"What do you think the president is going to do about the chemical attack in Syria?" asked Cliff.

Even just hearing the questions made me feel tainted by the world. This was exactly the kind of information I was supposed to be keeping out of my head, keeping away from my sensitive spirit. I found I had to put on my headphones most of the day, but as I didn't have any MoTab music stored, I ended up not being able to listen to anything at all. The headphones did keep my coworkers from addressing me, though, so they weren't entirely useless.

"We're having sandwiches for dinner?" I asked when I sat down at the table with my family that night.

"They don't require a recipe," Sally explained.

"You don't remember how to make *anything* without a recipe?" I asked.

"I know how to make sandwiches."

I was miffed at Sally throughout most of the meal, and she was miffed at me. The kids ate in silence, responding in monosyllables to any questions I asked about their day. After dinner, we all retired to the living room. Leslie picked up the remote and then put it down again.

"This is boring," she said. I knew everyone wanted to watch *The Amazing Race* or *The Voice* or *Supergirl* or any of the other half dozen shows we watched together regularly. It felt like a member of the family had just died.

"Maybe we should read the scriptures together," I suggested.

No one said anything for a long moment.

"I think I'll go work on my homework," Leslie finally replied.

"Me, too," said Terry.

They trudged off to their rooms. If they were really doing their homework, of course, that would be good. I'd have to check in on them shortly to make sure they weren't sneaking some time on their cell phones.

"Don't check too hard," Sally suggested.

"Maybe just a quick peek?" I returned.

Sally shook her head.

I sighed and looked about the room. "So what do you want to do?" I asked her.

She shrugged. "Play a game?"

"We still have games?"

"The kids used to play Sorry and Backgammon. I believe those are still in the closet. Want me to go check?"

We played five games of checkers.

"I think I'll go on to bed," Sally said around 8:45.

"This early?"

"I think so."

I stood up as she did. "You in the mood for…?" What other reason would someone want to go to bed early?

"Not tonight, dear."

"Okay."

I sat on the sofa staring at the blank television screen. I moved my arms and waved so I could see my reflection. Nowhere near as exciting as an actual show. I picked up the latest issue of the *Ensign*, but I'd already read all the articles I was interested in. Then I picked up the book by Dallin H. Oaks that Sally was reading, but after half a page I put it back down. I walked down the hall and stuck my head in the kids' rooms. Terry was playing a computer game and Leslie was reading a book.

"What's the book, young lady?"

She showed me the cover. *The Autobiography of Parley P. Pratt.*

"Good girl." Though the way she was holding the book, she might still be hiding something else.

"Biographies are more interesting than doctrine," she said a little defensively, and I again wondered what was up.

I decided, however, it wouldn't do to be too suspicious. Sally had told me this morning when I was quizzing the kids on their plans for the day that they should get a pass on some of this stuff. It was our job as parents to teach them correct principles and let them govern themselves. The most effective way we could do it was by setting the proper example.

"So you won't sneak in *Ellen* this afternoon?" I'd asked.

Sally raised an eyebrow and I kissed her goodbye.

Wednesday, though, work began to grow more frustrating. I needed a break from thinking of nothing else but my job, and yet I couldn't take a break. I understood this meant I was probably addicted to modern media, and it might be healthy to wean myself from it, perhaps permanently. I could ask the bishop what he thought after conference on Sunday. But as it was, I was irritable and snapped at two of my coworkers.

My boss pulled me aside at lunch. "Everything okay at home?"

I had to put my headphones back on after lunch to reduce human contact as much as possible.

Since I wasn't allowed to call Sally, I made an executive decision to stop by Japanese Garden and pick up some teriyaki for dinner. After all, restaurants weren't media. But when I arrived home, I discovered Sally had prepared meatballs and spaghetti.

"Smells wonderful," I said. "I can have the teriyaki for lunch tomorrow." I didn't see how I could be any more accommodating, but I still got the evil eye.

Sally didn't have much to say during dinner. Terry and Leslie continued to answer questions in monosyllables. Of course, being teenagers, this might have nothing to do with the fast, though they did both seem a little more taciturn than usual. They ran off to their rooms immediately after the meal was over. "Want to play checkers?" I asked Sally.

"Not really."

"Want to go for a walk?"

"It's too hot."

I grinned. "Want to take a shower together?"

Sally picked up the remote and pointed it at the television. "I want to watch *Dancing with the Stars*."

I took the remote from her hand, wondering if I should hide it or take it to work with me to reduce the temptation she felt when she was home alone. "*We* could dance," I suggested, taking her hand.

"To *God of our Fathers*?"

She might have a point there.

Things deteriorated as the week dragged on. I couldn't Google anything. I couldn't ask Siri questions I needed answered. I couldn't use my GPS to get around a detour. Instead of reading gospel literature, Sally and I kept retiring to bed earlier and earlier.

Leslie still seemed okay with reading Church books, or at least making the pretense, and Terry, of course, already had his freedom with the computer games. I kept trying to think of a way that *NCIS* or *Shots Fired* related to my job but couldn't think of any.

Friday night, Sally and I were in bed by 8:15. Even she was bored enough by now to agree to sex, and I made sure to take my time. Foreplay alone lasted almost an hour. Maybe this media fast would turn out all right, after all.

We'd long since fallen asleep when around 11:00, a siren woke us up. "Wh-what's that?" Sally mumbled, squinting her eyes when I turned on the light.

Another siren started to blare, and another. They sounded like air raid sirens. We got up and went to the window. Most of our neighbors were at their windows, too. It sounded like sirens were going off all over the city. But the sky was clear over Dallas. No tornado threat. What in the world could it be?

"We've got to turn on the TV," Sally said, heading for the bedroom door.

"No," I said. "This is a test. We have to stay strong. Stay true."

"Kent, it's not actually a commandment from God not to use any modern media. It's just something the stake president said. What if there's a gas leak? Or an escaped convict? Or something worse?"

I pointed out the window. "No one's leaving," I said. "So it can't be that urgent. Heavenly Father will protect us for being obedient."

"What if it's Syria or Russia attacking us in retaliation for bombing the Syrian airport yesterday?" Sally clapped a hand over her mouth.

I couldn't believe my own ears. "You've been watching the news?" I asked.

Sally dropped her hand and stomped her foot. "The sin is in *not* knowing what's going on in the world. It's not responsible."

The sirens finally stopped blaring. "See?" I said. "Everything's fine."

"You don't know that."

"Can't you feel the Spirit, Sally? Can't you?"

Sally stomped her foot again. "No, I can't. I don't feel any more spiritual than I normally do. If anything, I feel less spiritual."

I nodded. "Perhaps that's because you aren't following priesthood counsel."

Sally walked back over to the bed, grabbed a pillow, and thrust it at me. "Go feel spiritual on the sofa," she said.

Saturday was a long day, no office work to do from home, nothing fun to keep me occupied, nothing to say to my wife. I weeded the yard for a couple of hours and fixed the gutter I'd been meaning to get to for ages. Sally prepared sandwiches again for dinner. She went to the bedroom and locked the door right after Leslie loaded the dishwasher.

I decided to sneak to my study and turn on the computer for just a moment. I scrolled through the news, absorbing everything as quickly as I could. Someone had hacked into the Civil Defense warning system here in the city but setting off the sirens was apparently just a prank of some kind. There was a bombing in a Baghdad marketplace that killed forty-six people. A plane had made an emergency landing in Denver but everyone was okay. A mudslide in Ecuador had killed two hundred people.

I sat back in my chair and sighed in relief. My nerves felt energized. This was the way caffeine used to make me feel when I was a boy, before my dad forbade us to drink Coke anymore.

Media was an addiction. There was no doubt. The stake president was right to make us give it up.

But what good was it to do that for just one week? We'd be on the computer again or watching TV every second of the day starting Monday. Perhaps it was the Amish who were on to something.

The Amish.

I thought about the FLDS as I sat and stared at the computer for a long while.

Finally, I looked at my watch. It wasn't quite 7:00. I walked down the hall, banging on doors. "Everyone out!" I shouted. "Everyone out!"

Leslie and Terry opened their doors cautiously. I banged another time on Sally's door, and she finally opened as well.

"Everyone get dressed," I said. "We're going to the movies."

"What?"

"Really?"

"Huh?"

"How does everybody feel about that new science fiction flick, *Life*?"

Sally and the kids seemed too excited to care what we were seeing, as long as we were seeing *something*.

We bought ice cream on the way home and stayed up late playing an online trivia game, the boys against the girls.

And we skipped ward conference on Sunday, sitting in the living room together and binge-watching *Scandal* instead.

The Tree of Li(f)e

It was the last day of Girls Camp, and I was ready to go home, but our leaders had one final adventure for us to experience. We'd already had the fun of competing at scripture chases, learning to crochet, and standing up in front of everyone detailing what we thought our temple marriages would be like.

I'd asked my mom to send me to band camp, but she'd heard about the flute scene in some raunchy comedy and refused to even consider it. Then I'd asked to attend soccer camp, but she'd said soccer wasn't ladylike. So here I was in the woods.

If it had been Girl Scout camp, that might have been okay.

"I'm hungry," Brenda whispered. She was my best friend from Young Women. Well, to be honest, she was my *only* friend at church. Brenda wanted to be a pharmacist when she grew up. I wanted to be a psychiatrist or, if I couldn't get into med school, at least a psychologist. The other girls all wanted to be wives and mothers. Nothing wrong with that, of course. In fact, I wanted the same thing. It just wasn't *all* I wanted.

My mom said I thought too much. For her, that was a bad thing. For Mrs. Kavanaugh, my English teacher, it was good.

For my Sunday School teacher, it wasn't even an option. "Thinking leads to doubt," Sister Keenan said, "and once you start doubting, you're already too deceived to be saved."

So I didn't think too much about church. That strategy seemed to have worked well enough so far.

"Quiet down, girls," said Sister Moyes. She was the Beehive instructor, mine and Brenda's teacher, so I knew her best out of all the adults here. "We'll eat after this one last activity. Now follow me."

The fourteen girls taking part in Girls Camp trailed dutifully behind Sister Moyes and Sister Bonner. Sister Grisham followed at the rear, making sure no one lagged behind. We walked deep into the woods where there was no longer any trail. I kept a sharp eye out for poison ivy. And snakes. Wasn't Girls Camp supposed to be safe, I thought? The mere presence of an adult wasn't going to keep a bear at bay.

But maybe the prayer we offered this morning would.

"Here we are, girls." Sister Moyes pointed to a rope tied around a tree which led off through the woods until it reached another tree, and then led off still farther beyond that. "Sister Grisham, get out the blindfolds."

Brenda looked at me with a frown, and I could tell this wasn't going to be a particularly fun way to end the week. But I allowed Sister Grisham to tie the blindfold across my eyes. I was then directed to the rope. Susan was in front of me, Brenda behind me, with Marian after her.

"Ooh, Zoey," Brenda whispered to me. "I'm afraid."

"It'll be okay," I whispered back. "They won't let us get lost."

"Tommy was attacked by hornets at the Father/Son outing."

"Sister Moyes won't let anything bad happen to us."

"Does she have power over Nature?" Brenda countered. "It's not like she has the priesthood or anything." Perhaps I should suggest she become a lawyer rather than a pharmacist.

"Well, Brother Carson is back at the campsite." We always had at least one priesthood holder to supervise the women leaders.

"Fat lot of good that does us now."

"Just think about the juicy hamburgers waiting for us at the end."

I could hear Brenda rustling in the leaves behind me. "Okay, Zoey, okay."

"All right, girls," Sister Bonner announced. "I'm going to read Lehi's Dream to you from 1 Nephi." In a somber voice, she proceeded to read the vision we'd all heard a hundred times already in church, about Lehi traveling through a dark and dreary wilderness, only able to find his way by holding fast to the iron rod.

Some people were distracted by a large and spacious building and all the people inside who were laughing and having a good time, but Lehi persisted and made it to the Tree of Life, which had the most delicious fruit. Those who wandered away from the iron rod were lost in the wilderness or drowned in a river. Only those who held onto the rod were saved.

"So you girls have to make it to the Tree of Life, where we'll have a delicious fruit salad for lunch. Don't let go of the iron rod under any circumstances. Follow the iron rod and you'll always be safe. Any questions?" I raised my hand but couldn't tell if anyone was able to see me or not. "Yes, Zoey?" Sister Bonner asked.

"Why is this iron rod so limp?" There was a twitter among the other girls.

I could hear Sister Bonner sigh. "You need this lesson more than anyone else," she said. "Judging from how poorly you did in the scripture chase, I'll bet you don't even read your Book of Mormon every day."

She was right about that.

I'd also worn a sleeveless top to Sunday School once last month, and Sister Keenan had threatened to bring a potato sack to make me wear if I ever did that again. "I'll cut arm and leg holes in the sack and bring it with me every week from now on," she said.

"Wouldn't a potato sack with arm holes cut out still be sleeveless?" I asked.

I had to talk to the bishop after class that day. I didn't really mean to be a pain in the butt. I wanted to be a good girl. In fact, I wanted to be a great girl. A great woman. My mom insisted that coming to Girls Camp for a week would help me better myself. So I'd come along, though I'd bargained for a ticket to the Scripps Spelling Bee in return. Mom had shaken her head but agreed.

"Now, girls," Sister Bonner said, "start walking. Step carefully and slowly and don't let go of the iron rod no matter what."

I could hear rustling in front of me and figured the other girls were on the move, so I took a step forward. I heard a branch crack under my foot but kept going. "I hate this," Brenda muttered behind me.

"Let's just get it over with," I replied. I was thinking about the fruit salad waiting for us at the end of the activity. Not the substantial meal I was hoping for, of course. Brenda wasn't the only one who was hungry.

We walked on mostly in silence. A couple of the girls ahead of me giggled and whispered every once in a while. For some reason, we all seemed to feel it would be inappropriate to talk out loud. I could hear leaves rustling and twigs cracking. I brushed up against bushes, got stabbed in the side once by a large fallen branch, and tripped over a small log.

"Don't let go of the rope!" Sister Moyes shouted.

I felt around until my fingers touched the rope again, and I latched on more tightly. I contorted my face a couple of times, trying to force the blindfold away from my eyes just enough that I could cheat, but the blindfold was large and well secured. I heard Marian cry out in pain once, and Sister Grisham urged her to keep moving.

It seemed like ages before we even reached the first tree. The tree that had looked like it was only thirty feet away. This was going to be a long activity, I realized. I patted my way around the trunk and reached for the new rope leading us onward.

"Good, good," I heard Sister Bonner murmur. "You girls are doing just fine."

I thought about the point of the lesson, to teach us the importance of reading the scriptures. But if Heavenly Father truly wanted us to learn important life lessons from them, why did he make them so boring? The Young Women leaders went out of their way to make all our activities interesting and understandable.

They *wanted* us to learn from every single task they assigned over the past week. Even roasting marshmallows had somehow been imbued with meaning. But it seemed Heavenly Father went out of his way to make learning difficult.

Even difficulty wasn't the biggest problem. I was in Honors math, taking an extra hard algebra course, but that was challenging, which wasn't the same thing as difficult. And it certainly wasn't boring. Boring was not an incentive. Good teachers were anything but boring.

Wasn't Heavenly Father supposed to be perfect?

I felt something land on my arm and jerked quickly to make it fly off. I brushed up against another bush and hoped I didn't get Lyme disease. The good news was that the Young Women's budget was pretty low. I was sure the sisters couldn't afford to buy much rope. This would all be over soon.

Suddenly, off to our right, I heard a click, and music started playing. Ariana Grande's voice filled the air. Then the music was turned low and I could hear Sister Bonner whisper softly above it. "Let go of the rope," she said. "Come over this way. Over here we have music and Coca-Cola."

No one in the group, of course, was dumb enough to let go of the rope. Well, I assumed as much, anyway, even if I couldn't see for sure. Sister Bonner's whispered temptation continued, but we all kept plugging forward. This wasn't even a real test, I thought. We *knew* not to let go of the rope if we wanted to get through this, have lunch, and get home.

A couple of trees later, I heard Sister Grisham's voice off to the left. "There's food over here. Just let go and come eat." I heard her shake a bag of chips, tear it open, and munch down on something crunchy. I giggled.

"You think this is funny, young lady?" Sister Moyes demanded.

"I was remembering something that happened at home the other day."

"Keep your mind on the gospel," she returned tartly.

Whatever.

I thought about the last General Conference, being forced to watch every session at home dressed in my Sunday best. The prophet had looked so frail. His brief talk had sounded disjointed and forced. I watched the other members of the First Presidency and the Twelve on the stand as various leaders spoke before the crowd. Not a one of them nodded off, surprising for such old people. Or maybe I simply missed it because I was nodding off, too. But Dad made us take notes, and after every session was over, we had to give a summary of each talk.

If Heavenly Father really wanted us to learn, would he make Conference so tedious? It was even worse than Sacrament meeting. And that was saying something.

Even learning to crochet was exciting in comparison.

Another branch scratched my arm, and I almost cursed. I stopped and let go of the rope for just a moment to feel my arm. The branch had drawn blood. Darnation. Was it so gol-danged important that we stay off a real trail to learn our lesson? I couldn't wait to get home, take a shower, and get back to my books. I was reading *Twilight* at the moment.

Now there was a Mormon book I could get behind. Feeling blindly about me, I stubbed my toe on a root. I gritted my teeth and managed to grab hold of the rope again.

"That's good," I heard Sister Moyes whisper. "Hold to the rod, the iron rod."

I wondered if she was close enough to hit if I swung my arm out. It was too hard to gauge, so I just took another step forward instead. This couldn't go on much longer. They'd made their point. I wanted to eat.

"Zoey," Brenda whispered behind me, "give me a heads up next time you come across briars."

"Sorry."

Suddenly, off to the left, we heard something large crashing through the bushes followed by a loud growl. A couple of the girls squealed in terror, but I was pretty sure bears didn't growl in alto. I kept plodding forward.

After what seemed an eternity, I could sense we were out of the woods and in a clearing. More light was coming through the blindfold, and I stopped tripping over branches. There was a fresh breeze. A few feet farther on, Sister Grisham said, "Stop right there, girls. Now you just have to wait for a while before we do anything else. No talking whatsoever or you don't get lunch. Stand here in complete silence and contemplate your relationship with Heavenly Father and the scriptures."

Yeah, I thought, *that* wouldn't put us to sleep.

A couple of minutes later, the sound of the Mormon Tabernacle Choir drifted across the clearing from what seemed a far distance.

Where was Ariana Grande when you needed her?

Two minutes passed. Then five. Then ten. This was *really* getting tiresome. I felt the rope grow taut at times and then slack and then taut again and then slack. The choir was still singing softly. "Come, Come, Ye Saints" right now. I tried to make an intellectual exercise out of it.

How would a psychologist analyze the experience? Sensory deprivation sometimes led to enhanced emotional responses, I remembered reading somewhere. Was that why lunch had been delayed, too? Well, that wasn't really sensory deprivation, was it, I thought. I was absolutely feeling the sensation of hunger.

Five more minutes passed. Then ten. Then fifteen. What in the world were the leaders thinking?

The choir suddenly stopped singing. I heard Sister Bonner's voice from far away. "You can take off your blindfold now." Even in my relief, part of my brain registered the lack of a plural in that command. Odd, I thought.

I pulled off my blindfold. Brenda wasn't behind me. Susan wasn't in front of me. I was the only girl left still holding onto the rope. The others were thirty feet away, standing with the adults next to a table on which sat a portable CD player and several bowls of food. I let go of the rope and started over.

"You were the only girl who didn't instinctively know to come to the sound of the angels singing," said Sister Moyes. "Why do you think that is?"

My face felt hot. I didn't understand what was going on. Sister Grisham motioned to the other girls, and they hungrily began digging into the food. "Why didn't you come to the Tree of Life?" Sister Moyes asked.

Because I was holding onto the damn iron rod, I wanted to say, but I felt too confused to speak. I looked at the other girls, Brenda scarfing down the fruit salad, Marian thirstily drinking a glass of apple juice. They had learned something from this experience that had escaped me, I realized. And I was usually an A student.

How did they *know* what to do?

They must have been feeling the Spirit, I thought. Something I couldn't seem to accomplish. I had gotten lost even while keeping to the path.

"What have you learned today, Zoey?" asked Sister Moyes. Sisters Bonner and Grisham were staring at me intently, the hint of a smile on their lips. I felt a flash of anger.

The most obvious thing to learn, I thought furiously, was that following the rules got you nowhere. I always did everything I was supposed to do but still seemed to end up the black sheep.

Well, I did *almost* everything, I conceded, but then who was perfect? I tried to calm down and not act like a child, hoping to brush this all off. The iron rod was just another potato sack.

"Well?" Sister Moyes insisted.

I opened my mouth but then closed it again. I *had* learned something, I realized. I had learned that these people not only believed boredom was a good teaching tool but that humiliation was as well. My algebra teacher didn't behave like that, even when I got the question wrong.

So was I wrong to learn now? I didn't *want* to learn anything from this experience. It would be admitting that they were right.

But I learned I couldn't trust Brenda. I learned that although I was only thirteen, I would never be coming back to Girls Camp again, Scripps ticket or no Scripps ticket.

With a surprisingly deep feeling of disappointment, I think I also learned I'd never understand God, and I wondered for the first time if there was even a God out there worth understanding to begin with.

Wouldn't God know at least as much as my algebra teacher? I felt a sudden desire to do better in class.

The thing I learned which made me saddest of all, though, was that I might never understand the human mind, no matter how many degrees I had behind me. Kudos for that, Sister Moyes, kudos for that. Maybe all I was cut out for was motherhood, after all.

"Answer me, young woman!"

What could I say now that wouldn't get me in trouble with my parents? Mom still might keep me from the spelling bee if I got a bad report. I looked behind me at the rope hanging motionless between the last tree and a post in the middle of the clearing. A small, brown and white bird hopped sideways along its span.

"I learned that wild animals growl in alto," I said. Then I walked the rest of the way over to the table, grabbed a bowl of fruit salad, and began to eat.

None of the other girls spoke to me during lunch, not then and not later on the long, boring ride home.

The Organ Donor

"Thank you for the lovely message," Laura said, standing up. "I'm truly blessed to have faithful Home Teachers like you." Brother Franklin and Brother Shea smiled. They stood up as well.

"We think *you're* the faithful one," Brother Franklin replied, "asking your husband to move out until he repents and is rebaptized."

Laura grimaced, not wanting to think again about Todd's descent into masturbation and pornography, which had led to that fateful tryst with a masseuse who did more than rub his back. After his excommunication, Todd swore absolute fidelity, but Laura told him he couldn't come back until he'd completed his requisite year as a non-member obeying all the commandments so he could become a Latter-day Saint once more.

"A marriage can only succeed if one puts Heavenly Father ahead of one's spouse," she told the Home Teachers. Her mother had always put the Church first, she remembered, and her father knew it. Whenever he watched a football game on Sunday, her mother made him read aloud from the Book of Mormon for half an hour before she would cook for him again. Even the day of the Superbowl, her mother would set the remote on top of a copy of the Book of Mormon, just to remind him. He didn't watch football often.

Laura shook Brother Franklin's hand and then Brother Shea's and led the two men to the door. She saw Brother Shea take a long, last look at the organ in the living room and smiled. He'd been glancing at it during the entire visit. She thought about offering the instrument to him, not sure she ever wanted to hear the damn thing again, but instead she said, "You're welcome to come play any time." She considered a moment and then added, "As long as you bring Sister Shea." Laura knew she was an attractive woman and didn't want to cause grief for anyone else.

Why in the world hadn't she been enough for Todd?

"I may just do that," Brother Shea said with a laugh. "I may very well do that."

The men left and Laura locked the door behind them, letting her fingers rest on the imitation Salt Lake temple door handle face plates. She'd always told the children that theirs was a House of the Lord, too. She wondered if she should have the facsimiles replaced until Todd came back, but she was afraid of what the kids would think on the rare occasions they chose to visit. Both children were grown, Albert in his second year at BYU and Grace married and living in San Jose.

The house was so lonely now. She thought about moving from Santa Rosa to Salt Lake where she'd grown up. Most of her extended family was still there. It would be safer among more Mormons. Safer physically, of course, but also safer emotionally. She owed it to Todd, though, to give him a chance. And Bishop Ferdin had expressly forbidden her to move. "We need your tithing dollars right here," he said, laughing.

"But I don't pay tithing," she said. "I don't have a job."

"Yes, but your husband might stop paying if you left." The bishop laughed again. It was an odd comment, she thought, given that Todd attended another ward across town these days. Laura couldn't quite tell if the bishop was joking, but she knew he was the man she had to follow now that her husband no longer had the gift of the Holy Ghost. She decided to stay.

Laura went to the kitchen and poured herself a glass of grape juice. She liked orange juice for breakfast, apple juice in the afternoon, and grape juice in the evening. Variety was important to keep life interesting.

Laura frowned, thinking of the prostitute.

She turned off the kitchen light and headed for the back of the house to the bedroom, her footsteps echoing in the hallway. She climbed under the covers and turned on the television, the mattress so large without Todd. She considered that this must be what it felt like to be a widow, to know you were alone for now but would eventually be reunited with your husband if you were faithful and patient.

She wondered if waiting until the baptism was enough. Perhaps she should wait until they met again in the Celestial room of the temple before returning his key.

The last few minutes of *Father Brown* were playing. It was nice to see that at least a few Catholic priests were good people. Though even he didn't compare to Bishop Ferdin. The bishop had asked his own wife to bring her casseroles every night the first week after Todd's Court of Love. He'd ordered the Relief Society president to ask Laura's Visiting

Teachers to come every two weeks for the foreseeable future instead of just once a month. He made sure the High Priests Group Leader assigned the most reliable Home Teachers to her.

And he promised to find just the right calling for her at church so she'd feel needed and wanted and loved. To be honest, Laura wasn't quite sure she wanted a different calling. She'd been ward librarian for years. It was an easy job and let her spend an inordinate amount of time by herself, time she filled by writing poetry.

She always felt more inspired to write when at church. But she hadn't felt like writing anything at all ever since Todd's confession. As the weeks passed and no new calling came her way, Laura began to feel that maybe she *wasn't* needed, or wanted, or loved. Maybe Todd was right to seek affection elsewhere. Maybe his sins were all *her* fault.

On Saturday, Laura read the latest issue of the *Ensign* cover to cover, trying to make herself worthy of just the right position in the ward. She could feel Satan tempting her to blame Todd's behavior on the Church. As a member of the stake high council, he'd been away at meetings all the time. It was no wonder they'd grown apart.

She wished *she* could be called to the high council. Or the bishopric. Or the stake presidency. She'd change the way the whole system worked. She'd cut three-fourths of the extra hours members spent at church beyond the three-hour block. She'd assign talks on how to keep love in a marriage. Maybe she'd even start a special class that all married couples in the ward would be asked to attend together. She could use some of the ward's tithing money to hire a marriage counselor to teach the class.

If maintaining a successful temple marriage was the single most important commandment, it seemed odd that such a class wasn't already part of the Church curriculum. She would change that when she was called to the leadership.

Was it prideful to have good ideas?

If the Lord could have as much faith in Laura as she had in him, she reflected, she'd make the whole world a better place.

Or at least the ward.

Laura sat on the back porch in the sun and watched the neighbor's cat creep along the top of the fence separating their yards. He wasn't neutered and kept chasing other cats in the neighborhood. She watched as two hummingbirds fought over her hibiscus. She called Grace to chat for a few minutes. Then she called Albert, but he didn't answer. And she thought about Todd.

She'd considered killing him the night he confessed. Her husband was registered as an organ donor, she remembered thinking, and his death would not only free her from further association with him but would bless the lives of half a dozen other people as well. He'd already donated one organ, of course, that he should have kept to himself. She was so mad she wanted to cut it off. But then he'd cried and looked so pathetic she'd agreed to a year's separation.

She wondered if she could consider that part of her year's supply—a year's supply of peace.

Only she wasn't really at peace. She was tired of being cooped up in the library, tired of staring at a blank sheet of paper when words just wouldn't come. The bishop was definitely right. She needed a new calling. She'd so longed to be Seminary class president when she was a girl. But every year, a boy was called to the position instead and she was called upon only to offer the opening prayer a couple of times a week to invite the Spirit into the lesson.

She wanted something real this time, something that proved Heavenly Father liked her more than Todd did. If only she could be called to the General Relief Society and make changes that affected every woman in the entire Church. But she knew that was too much to dream for. She'd just have to accept something meaty here in the ward.

Laura heated up a Lean Cuisine for dinner, poured herself some grape juice, and watched two episodes of *As Time Goes By* in the bedroom. She wondered if there might be someone from her past she could rekindle a romance with.

It would have to be Todd, she realized with a half smile. He was in her past now, and he was the only man Laura had ever loved. But what good was it to love someone who didn't love you back? Todd would never be able to donate his heart when he died, she realized. He had no heart to give.

Did Heavenly Father love her back?

Please, she prayed, *find a place for me in the ward*. She felt like an inactive for the first time in her life, someone who knew deep down she was supposed to be singing hymns on Sunday but had no hymnbook to open. The scriptures were supposed to be an iron rod to hold onto, but they seemed to be rusting these days. She dreamed of being the new Relief Society president for the ward or the new Gospel Doctrine teacher, something realistic but important, something that would give her life meaning and prestige again.

She saw how people looked at her now because of what her husband had done.

As soon as Grace heard what had happened, she asked Laura to move in with her for a while. Laura wasn't sure she wanted to do that. She'd want to live on her own even if she did go to San Jose. She'd always dreamed of living in San Francisco, though. She'd be happy there even in a dump in a poor neighborhood. She wanted to sit along the beach and write poetry. Or read Emily Dickinson while sunning herself in Golden Gate Park.

But she had to be practical, and Salt Lake seemed the safest choice. She'd find a place within walking distance of the Church Office Building. Maybe back in Zion she really could be called to a churchwide position.

Sunday morning, Laura took a shower and put on her lavender dress with the petite bows on the sleeves. She sat all alone in the tiny library most of the morning, her solitude broken only by Sister Cooney, who needed to make copies, and Brother Talbot, who'd forgotten his priesthood manual. As she watched Brother Talbot walk away with his firm buttocks, she wondered if she should take Todd back before the year was up.

Perhaps she'd let him return at strategic intervals solely for the purpose of having him go down on her. He'd always resisted when she asked for it before, but he owed her now.

He'd service her for a change and then be sent back across town to take a cold shower.

Walking to the chapel for Sacrament meeting, Laura saw two sisters glance in her direction and whisper to each other. One mother instinctively pulled her daughter out of Laura's line of sight. Two of the high priests looked at her with blank expressions, probably mad she'd forced Todd to attend a different ward for the next year.

How could the bishop be so nice to her, she wondered, and the Visiting Teachers, and the Home Teachers, while everyone else acted like *she* was the one who'd been excommunicated? She saw Bishop Ferdin greeting people at the chapel doors and hoped he'd have some good news.

And he did. Heavenly Father cared even about the fall of a sparrow. "Sister Goodman," the bishop said, taking her hand, "come see me after services. I want to extend a calling to you." He smiled. "The *Lord* wants to extend a calling."

Laura hardly noticed the speakers during the meeting. The choir sang "A Poor Wayfaring Man of Grief" and a teenage girl said something about chastity for a few minutes, but for the most part, all Laura could think about was her new calling.

The Lord loved her. Life was going to be good again, perhaps even better than when Todd was still home. Unless, she thought suddenly, Heavenly Father felt the same way about her as most of the congregants in the ward did.

She frowned. As the hour wore on, she began to worry more and more. What if she was called to the Nursery? What if she was called to be den mother for the Cub Scouts? She did not want to travel any more deeply into the hinterlands.

"Come in, come in," the bishop said when Laura knocked on his office door ten minutes after the closing prayer. She sat down in a chair in front of his desk. "I've been praying and fasting for inspiration," Bishop Ferdin said. "I wanted to make sure to offer you the perfect calling, one that will address your needs but ours as well."

Relief Society president, Laura chanted to herself. *Relief Society president, Relief Society president.*

"I've been informed by the Holy Ghost that I should extend to you the calling of ward organist. Sister Perez is moving soon, and as the new organist, you'll be right up on the stage in front of everyone every Sunday. You'll get to spend time with the members of the choir. You know my wife is the choir director, and she tells me she really wants to work with you."

He sat back and smiled, but Laura's mind went blank like Joseph Smith's when he was given a fake seer stone. The air seemed to rush out of the room. She felt she'd just been dunked in the temple baptismal font and was being held down under the water. She couldn't breathe.

"I—I don't know what to say," Laura stammered.

"Sister Goodman, will you accept the Lord's call?"

Laura's heart was racing. This wasn't the way things were supposed to go at all. "But…but…"

"Sister Goodman," the bishop said softly, "I've prayed long and hard about this."

"But…I…"

"Yes?"

"But I don't know how to play the organ," she said.

Bishop Ferdin stared at her, his brows furrowed.

"Todd was the organist in the family," she explained. "He tried to teach the kids, but neither of them cared about learning. Even Todd hasn't played much the last few years. He…"

The bishop blinked but said nothing. Laura felt the world stop, the way Joseph Smith must have felt when he realized the first 116 pages of the Book of Mormon had been lost. She wanted Bishop Ferdin to say something else. She *needed* him to say something else. She looked at him and clasped her hands tightly.

After a moment, the bishop wiped his brow. He stared at the snow globe on his desk with the Salt Lake temple inside it. He turned to look at the framed portrait of the First Presidency on the wall beside him. He looked straight ahead at a spot on the wall behind Laura's head. He wiped his brow again.

"I…I guess I could always get Todd to teach me a few of the more popular hymns…"

Bishop Ferdin slapped the desk so hard the snow globe almost bounced off. "That's it!" he said. He breathed out heavily and smiled again. "The Lord has called you to this position to help you with your marriage. Yes. It's to help you with your marriage."

Laura looked at the bishop a long moment and then forced a smile. She looked at the snow globe, and at the portrait of the First Presidency, and then deep into Bishop Ferdin's eyes. The bishop offered his hand, Laura took it, and then she walked slowly out of the office. She walked down the long hallway to the foyer and past two women talking on the sofa.

She didn't notice if they whispered about her or not. She walked out through the glass doors to her car in the parking lot. She sat down behind the wheel and stared at the meetinghouse for a long moment. A crow squawked loudly when a child ran too close to where it was pecking at something on the ground.

When she arrived back at the house, Laura went to her computer and looked up Catholic Charities. No one would be in the office today, she expected, but she picked up the phone and dialed anyway. When the voice mail came on, she took a deep breath and left a message. "I have a Suzuki organ I'd like to donate," she said. "Please call me on Monday to arrange for a pickup."

Laura hung up the phone and changed out of her Sunday clothes into her favorite house dress. She went to the kitchen and put a Lean Cuisine in the microwave and poured herself a glass of apple juice. Then she sat down and started planning her move to San Francisco.

To Serve Man

"Hey, Logan," said Ethan, sticking his head above the partition separating our desks, "want to have lunch together again?"

I glanced at my watch. It was 11:45, just about the time I normally tried to head out. If I didn't reach the food court before noon, the lines were abominably long, eating into my half hour break. Ethan preferred later lunches, so I appreciated his effort to please. "Sure," I said. "Thai food sound okay?"

"Anything. I just need to get out of here for a few minutes."

I frowned and logged off my computer while Ethan logged off his. Lately, it seemed all we talked about was our problems, and it looked like he had another issue he wanted to discuss. Back when I'd been a missionary in Uruguay, I found that a lot of non-Mormons liked taking advantage of the opportunity to confess their sins to someone other than a Catholic priest.

Why they thought a nineteen-year-old kid from the U.S. was a better choice I never figured out, but it happened consistently. In my first few jobs after my mission, coworkers would pull me aside and discuss the most intimate details of their lives, even asking for sex advice from me, still a virgin. "You just have that kind of face," one of them told me.

Whatever that meant. Once, my boss asked for suggestions on how to discipline her sixteen-year-old daughter, who'd recently started smoking. As if I would have any clue. This kind of thing had continued at every job since.

Even neighbors would drop by for a private "chat" without their spouse. The faith people put in me could be kind of daunting. But I decided that if Heavenly Father made me seem approachable to people, I had to step up and help whenever I could.

It was late May in Seattle, which could sometimes still be cool, but today the high was supposed to be 81. I was surprised to see Ethan grab a light jacket as we headed out. "You okay, buddy?"

"Let's wait till we get our food."

A frumpy Asian woman scooped some pad thai into a pressed paper container for me and some spicy chicken on white rice in another for Ethan. An attractive Asian girl took our payment. I dropped two dollars in the tip jar and pointed Ethan toward the courtyard. We'd made it just in time. There were still a few tables left. I set my food down on a table partially in the shade, but Ethan shook his head and pointed to a table sitting in direct sunlight. I joined him at the other table.

"What's up, buddy?" I asked.

Ethan was sixty-four, only a year away from retirement, while I was still in my early thirties, not usually the best mixture for a friendship. But he was the sole equity loan underwriter at the credit union and I was the sole equity loan processor, so we'd grown relatively close over the past couple of years.

Ethan had told me about his daughter's troubled marriage and his son's inability to find a good job. I'd told him about my son insisting someone other than me baptize him and my daughter wanting priesthood blessings only from the bishop. Ethan had told me about his ailing wife, and I'd told him about my divorce from Janelle.

"Everyone thinks you're so good," Janelle had told me, "but I know the truth." The same thing she said to the kids about me every day. I didn't know what more she wanted. I was an RM, I'd graduated from BYU, I attended church weekly, and I paid my tithing.

"But you believe in evolution," Janelle had complained. "You believe it's okay for people to get tattoos. I've smelled coffee on your breath. I need to be with someone who will lead me to the Celestial Kingdom."

Ethan hadn't fully understood the situation, but he always listened patiently when we talked. When I explained the ramifications of a temple divorce, he told me the God he believed in would never keep me away from the people I loved in the next life.

I did still love Janelle, and if we both ended up making it all the way to the top degree of heaven, I felt sure our divorce could be annulled. A reverse Dustin Hoffman and Katharine Ross.

A movie I hadn't seen until after the divorce. It may have only had a PG rating, but everyone knew it was about adultery and showed brief flashes of nudity. No good Mormon would watch such a film.

But I was still a good Mormon. I still read my scriptures every day. I prayed every day. I did my genealogy. I gave talks in Sacrament meeting whenever I was asked. And I'd laminated a card which said, "Inasmuch as ye have done it unto one of the least of these my brethren, ye have done it unto me." I carried it in my shirt pocket and read it at least once every day on my way to work.

"It's Lupita," Ethan said, stabbing a bite of chicken forcefully.

"Is she getting worse?"

He shook his head. "She's still the same. It's just that…"

"Yes?" I forked a wad of noodles into my mouth.

"I've told you we never have sex anymore."

"Yes," I said.

"I've been good," said Ethan. "I've been faithful. But now…"

I took a sip of my Coke. "Are you having an affair?"

"That's the problem," he said. "I'm not. But I want to. Very badly." He smiled wistfully and shook his head. "The doctor says I have cancer," he continued. "I've probably got less than a year to live."

"Ethan, I'm sorry." I set my fork down and put my hand on his arm. He looked at it for a moment but didn't pull away.

At church, I made a point of hugging my male friends rather than offer the routine handshake. It was my attempt at subversion. I wanted Mormons to stop feeling so threatened by affection between males.

I was sure that since Janelle had divorced me, some of the ward members suspected the reason was my sexual orientation. But I went on hugging them, anyway. It was a real service to stamp out homophobia, I thought, whatever gossip it might inspire.

When it came up in conversation that I didn't drink and people subsequently wondered if I was in AA, I'd just ask them, "What does the second A stand for?" and leave it at that. It seemed to me an insult to recovering alcoholics to feel the need to deny I was one, even if the truth was I'd never had so much as a single drink yet.

"Logan, I want to live while I'm alive," Ethan went on. "Is that such a terrible thing?" He stabbed another bite of chicken as if trying to keep it from escaping.

I thought about all the casseroles Janelle had baked for sick members of the ward, the funeral potatoes when someone died. "What can I do for you?" I asked. As Elders Quorum president, I was used to helping members pack up and move. I was used to mowing the lawns of sick congregants.

But I hated doing the standard service projects. I wanted to teach someone's son how to play the clarinet. I wanted to interest the Elders Quorum in forming a book club. I wanted to convince the ward choir to sing "Brighter Than the Sun" to my depressed second counselor. But I sensed Ethan was going to need something more meaningful than any of that.

Did he want me to find him a hooker?

Why was that the first thing that came to my mind?

"I feel suffocated, Logan. It's been six years since I've had sex with Lupita. I…I don't want to spend the rest of my life like that." He stared at a young woman disposing of a half-eaten salad. "The rest of my life…"

I felt pretty frustrated, too, now that Janelle and I no longer shared a bed. I beat off almost every night, which I was sure Ethan did, too, but there was always hope I'd find someone else. That wasn't a possibility for Ethan. "What are you going to do?" I asked.

In addition to small but regular donations to groups like Fare Start and the Northwest Harvest Food Bank, I also made a point of keeping lots of single dollar bills in my wallet. I gave out five of them to homeless people every day on my way to the light rail station after work. But those kinds of things had such a small impact on the quality of someone's life.

Even helping people get equity loans so they could pay for upgrades on their homes or for their child's education seemed too remote an act. I wanted something that was the emotional equivalent of a blood transfusion directly to the person I was attempting to serve. Anything less felt like saying, "I gave at the office."

Ethan shoved a large bite of chicken into his mouth and began chewing. I took another bite of my own lunch and waited for him to speak. "I don't want to hurt Lupita," he insisted.

"Then don't tell her."

Ethan stared at me, as shocked, apparently, as I was at what I'd just said. Extramarital sex was a sin. Even for non-Mormons. So why did suggesting such a thing make me feel closer to Ethan?

"She gets so suspicious," he said. "She knows I'm a red-blooded man and have natural human urges. So anytime I'm away from the house for long, she worries. I don't want to upset her. We watch a lot of TV, and I read to her sometimes. Some nights, we sing karaoke in the bedroom. I do enjoy her company, even now. But it's not enough."

I rubbed my chin for a moment. I discovered I had a drop of sauce on my face, so I grabbed my napkin and wiped it off. Then I mused for another moment.

In my calling at church, I had to make Home Teaching assignments, trying to match up personalities that would get along. I had to guess which men were flowers waiting to bloom—or cucumbers waiting to sprout—and cajole them into teaching a priesthood lesson that would help them as much as the rest of the quorum. Elders who were afraid to go to the bishop about their concerns with Church history or doctrine would come to me first.

"You're so easy to talk to," they said. But I never felt I was serving them appropriately. Two of them ended up going inactive. Another ended up resigning from the Church.

All I'd done was be honest.

Maybe honesty wasn't always useful.

Just ask Joseph Smith, I thought.

Or Boyd K. Packer.

"So what you need," I said slowly, "is someone to come to your house who won't arouse Lupita's suspicion."

Ethan laughed, a note of resignation in his voice. "How could *any* woman come to my house and not upset Lupita?" he said. Then he sighed heavily. "I don't know that I even need full-fledged sex. I could probably get by with just a blow job once in a while." He looked at me nervously as if afraid he'd said too much.

I thought of an old *Twilight Zone* episode I'd seen as a boy. Aliens arrive on Earth and seem to have nothing but the welfare of humans in mind. Scientists manage to translate the title of one of their books, but it's the only bit of written language they're able to decipher. The book is called *To Serve Man*. Astounded that the aliens really do have the best interests of humans as their motivation, thousands of Earthlings agree to make a trip to the aliens' home planet.

Only after it's too late do humans translate the rest of that magnanimous book. Turns out it's a cookbook.

I needed to do something which made me feel that even now, with my family in tatters, I was still a good and decent person. This, of course, made whatever generosity I intended to offer Ethan a selfish act rather than an altruistic one. Then again, since every time Mormons did a good deed, they jotted it down on the resumés they were submitting for entrance into the Celestial Kingdom, perhaps that was already the case.

I wanted to do something that would legitimately serve Ethan, something which required a tangible sacrifice. Only one option seemed viable. "How would you feel about getting a blow job from a guy?" I asked.

Ethan's eyebrows rose half an inch. "Well, I'm not gay," he replied carefully. "I'm not even bi."

I nodded. "I'm straight, too." What difference did that make? I didn't want to date him.

Ethan looked at me with his brows furrowed, pushing his fork gently into another bite of chicken.

"I could come to your place once or twice a week," I said. "You could tell Lupita we wanted to bitch about our manager but didn't feel safe doing it at work. Or you could tell her we're just friends and want to hang out in your garage once in a while. Or whatever."

"Or whatever," he repeated.

I should feel repulsed by what I was saying, I thought. I should feel guilty. Such behavior would force me to confess to the bishop. Would get me excommunicated. And yet I didn't feel the slightest need to repent.

Why would anyone ever need to repent of sincere service to their fellow man?

I didn't like cleaning the chapel once a month, but I did it.

I remembered what I liked about Janelle's blow jobs, and what I didn't. Maybe if I'd done this years ago, I thought, I'd have been better able to understand Janelle's concerns on that score. Perhaps it was Ethan who was doing me a favor.

"I can stop by tonight if that works for you," I said.

Ethan smiled for the first time today. "You're a real pal, Logan." He reached across the table and slapped me on the shoulder. I slurped up some more of my pad thai, and Ethan gently scooped up another bite of chicken. "Is there anything I can do for *you*?" he asked.

Service, I thought, shouldn't be so self-serving. But that didn't keep me from answering. "Does your daughter have any single friends?"

Ethan laughed so loudly that the people at the next table looked over at us. "I'll see what I can do, Logan," he said. "I'll see what I can do."

We stood up and deposited our cartons into the appropriate waste receptacles. There was a fresh breeze running down Third Avenue which prevented the sun from beating down. But Ethan pulled off his jacket as we started back for the credit union. We logged onto our computers and got back to work.

Exit Interview

I stepped off the bus, picked a yellow wildflower growing in the parking strip, and walked the last five blocks to the Emersons' house. Today marked the one-week anniversary of my first job after graduating with a degree in Early Childhood Education from Florida State University. I'd considered working in a Montessori school or in a public kindergarten, but I wanted the close contact of interacting with a limited number of children in a more intimate setting.

I loved being a nanny to four-year-old Heather and five-year-old Tina. And the Emersons seemed like a nice couple. They had a painting of Jesus coming out of the clouds on one wall and a huge picture of some church with multiple spires on another. They asked me to have the girls say a prayer before each meal, and they asked me to read at least one Bible story to them out of a children's book every day.

I didn't remember the one about God touching stones to make them glow, but then, I'd never paid much attention the few times my parents took me to church. The girls were angels, though, so the parents must have been doing something right. The Emersons' house was large, even by the standards of this middle-class community. The girls had separate bedrooms, and there was an empty room waiting for a third child due in a couple of months.

My own family had been less than ideal, my parents splitting when I was ten, my mother bringing men over to spend the night even before my dad moved out.

They hadn't fought, though. Not over that, anyway. Their arguments were usually about capital punishment or unions or nuclear energy.

Still, I always knew my parents loved me. I was just never sure I was a high priority for them.

Another fun aspect of my first job was discovering how pleasant it was to work in a clean neighborhood, not at all like the one where I lived. I'd passed two neighbors washing their cars this morning. Another neighbor was carefully weeding a flower patch. Smiling to myself, I started to slip my key into the lock when suddenly the door swung open, startling me. I dropped the key and bent to pick it up.

"Good morning, Melinda," I said, greeting the children's mother. I could see Dustin behind her. "Good morning, Dustin." He'd usually left for work by this time. It was Friday, though, so perhaps he was taking the day off so we could all do something together as a family. That would be fun.

"Hello, Margaret," Melinda replied in a subdued voice. "Come in." Uh-oh, I thought. Someone must be sick. I tried to remember if I'd given either of the girls leftovers which might have been left in the fridge too long.

I walked into the kitchen and put my bag down. "How are the girls this morning?"

"Please sit," Melinda said, motioning toward the table. All three of us sat down. The chairs screeching across the tile sounded abnormally loud.

It was clear something was wrong. Had one of the girls told them I'd been mean? I couldn't recall getting angry this week, even when the kids did naturally annoying things any child might do, which didn't happen often. They laughed a lot, rarely argued, and weren't especially messy.

And I was way too excited about my first job to let anything get to me yet. Tina had accidentally spilled orange juice on me the day before, but that was nothing to get upset about. I certainly hadn't spanked her or anything. I didn't believe in corporal punishment.

"What is it?" I asked.

Melinda and Dustin exchanged glances. They looked down at their hands and then at me and then at each other. Melinda opened her mouth to speak, but Dustin beat her to it. "We looked in the trash yesterday," he said, "and we found an empty bottle of kombucha tea."

I frowned. "Yes?"

"You know we're Mormons, don't you?" asked Dustin.

"Yes?" They'd told me that during our first interview, though I hadn't thought much about it. What difference did something like that make?

"We can't have you bringing tea into the house."

"Oh," I said. "Okay. I didn't know. I won't do it again."

Melinda and Dustin exchanged glances again. "That's not all, Margaret."

I didn't understand what was going on. I'd clearly offended them in some manner but couldn't imagine how. I'd even brought the girls little gifts yesterday. Perhaps that was it. Their parents felt I was overstepping my bounds. I hated finding out I'd done something wrong. I clutched my wildflower tightly. "Yes?" I said.

"We looked on the bottle," said Melinda. "Kombucha tea contains alcohol. You brought alcohol to our house and drank it while you were at work." She took a deep breath. "While supervising our children."

I almost laughed but instinctively knew to suppress the reaction. It would have been nervous laughter in any event, not something which might lighten the mood. "Kombucha contains less than 1% alcohol," I said. "They sell it to kids. You don't have to be eighteen. It's a probiotic sold with other health drinks."

"Heather said you let her taste it."

"I won't bring any tea over again."

"You gave our daughter alcohol."

Now I started to get scared. Were they going to report me for child abuse? I might never get another job. I might go to jail.

Over kombucha tea.

"Vanilla extract has a lot more alcohol," I said. "And no one is getting drunk eating ice cream. But I get it. If you were vegans and I brought over a ham sandwich or beef jerky, you'd be upset. I just didn't know. Now I know. It won't happen again."

Melinda and Dustin looked at each other once more. "It's not just the tea," said Dustin. "You also came to work one day with coffee breath. Apparently, there's been a series of unacceptable behaviors."

I frowned again. I hadn't stolen anything, hadn't looked in any cabinets to snoop. I hadn't even called my boyfriend from the house. I'd cleaned up after the children meticulously. I'd taught Heather the alphabet. "I don't understand."

"You'll still be drinking that tea in your own home, won't you?" asked Dustin. "And coffee?"

"Yes?"

"So you'll still be setting a bad example for the girls."

I blinked and tried to refocus. They were going to tell me what I could and couldn't do in my own home? More than surprising, their complaints were patently ridiculous, but whatever. They were worried about their children. That was a good thing. Lots of parents weren't. But I didn't want to get fired from my very first job.

I could lie if I had to, not admirable, I supposed, but while there were other nanny jobs out there, most of them had been scooped up right after graduation.

"I don't *have* to keep drinking kombucha," I said. "It's not like it's addictive or anything. If you prefer I don't drink it, I don't have to drink it. I won't drink coffee anymore, either. Makes me hyper anyway."

"The problem," said Melinda carefully, "is that you're asking us to trust you."

"When you've already proven you're untrustworthy," Dustin added.

I'd graduated with a 3.8 average. I had letters of recommendation from three of the toughest teachers in my department. I didn't have any tattoos or piercings, other than the normal ones in my ears. My hair was its natural color, mousy brown. I took a deep breath. We needed a change of topic or I was going to get angry, and that wouldn't help anyone, especially me. "You said there were other problems?"

"You told the girls to wash their hands regularly," said Dustin.

My jaw dropped but I tried to recover and not show my shock any longer than necessary. Did he really just say that? I must have misunderstood. Maybe there *was* too much alcohol in that tea. "You don't approve of me teaching hygiene?" I asked.

"The problem is that you told them using hand sanitizer promoted the evolution of resistant bacteria and that's why washing was better." Dustin shook his head. "It took a while for us to make out that Tina was saying 'evolution,' but you can't be teaching the children things which will make them doubt God."

My mouth fell open a second time. This time I made no effort to hide my dismay. When I saw Dustin and Melinda look at each other once again, I forced myself to say it. "There's *more*?"

It looked like almost anything could set these people off. I'd probably said "God bless you" after one of the girls sneezed, and I was going to be called out for taking the Lord's name in vain.

I'd heard about parents from hell and knew sooner or later I'd run across some, but I'd just have to bear with it for now if I was going to start building my resumé. In fact, in some ways, being able to tactfully mention I'd dealt with demanding parents might be a plus when seeking future employment.

If I could prove I'd met their demands.

The stem of my wildflower was mush.

Dustin spoke up again. "You brought a CD of *Phantom of the Opera* and had the girls listen to it."

"Yes?"

"We understand you're just trying to introduce them to the arts, but it's a story about a middle-aged man obsessing over a young woman." He paused, and he and Melinda exchanged glances yet again. "It's inappropriate."

Was *this* what the problem was all about? I was pretty, though not beautiful, and in good shape. Was Melinda jealous? She had no reason to be, of course. She was a lot prettier than I was. But some men fell in love with the nanny simply because she was young.

I didn't want my youth to be an obstacle, though. I'd never get to be Mrs. Doubtfire without a few decades of experience under my belt. And I could hardly get experience if mothers were going to feel threatened by me.

"And you came to work today with sleeves that can't be even two inches long. You're teaching our girls to dress in ways that provoke impure thoughts in men."

"Your girls are four and five."

Melinda sat up straight, and Dustin followed her example. The meeting was clearly coming to a close. I felt as if I'd taken a step off a front porch only to discover the stairs were missing. "So you see it's not just one thing," Melinda said.

"We really are tolerant people," Dustin continued, "but you simply are not cut out to work around young children."

"We won't be giving you a recommendation."

I sat there for a long moment, stunned. Surely, these people were behaving in an extreme manner, even for demanding parents. All Mormons couldn't be this strict. Perhaps Melinda and Dustin were having second thoughts about having anyone at all in their home, and their discomfort was coming out in this bizarre fashion.

Maybe it was just a hormone overload from Melinda's pregnancy. It really had nothing to do with me. They'd have found fault with any nanny. I just happened to be the one in their crosshairs.

"I suppose you'll want your key back." I started to reach for my pocket.

"Oh, no, dear," said Melinda with a smile, patting my arm. "We already changed the locks. You keep that as a reminder to be a better person."

Dustin and Melinda stood up, and I realized the meeting was officially over. "Can I at least say goodbye to the girls?"

Melinda shook her head sadly. "We don't think that would be a good idea."

Dustin walked over to the kitchen door and opened it. I picked up my bag and stepped outside, heading slowly back to the bus stop. It felt farther than five blocks. I dropped the wildflower back on the parking strip.

Unemployed after only a week. But perhaps this was better than being fired after three weeks or two months. I could probably avoid letting other potential employers know I'd had this first job at all.

I tried to remember some of the other postings I'd seen. There was that family who had the child with Down Syndrome. And that family with the deaf infant. Those jobs might still be available. Though I'd had my heart set on a family with more than one child. Perhaps that Hasidic family would hire me, if they accepted non-Jewish applicants. I could pretend I kept kosher.

Such infantile parents. Odd that none of my professors had even suggested the possibility existed.

The reason, I supposed, people needed experience in "the real world" to supplement their education.

Well, I was a quick learner. At least *my* parents had emphasized questioning.

Perhaps I'd call my dad tonight. We hadn't chatted in a while.

I pulled out my kombucha tea and took a swig. I thought about the one job opening I'd seen listed at the Montessori school and hoped it was still available. The bus arrived a few minutes later, and I climbed aboard, sitting next to a mother with a screaming infant. I looked out the window and stared at all the lovely houses as we passed by.

The Merit Badge

"Hurry up, Hank," my father ordered, jingling the car keys.

"What's the rush?" I asked. "The woods aren't going anywhere."

"We need to set up camp before dark," my father replied. "You don't want to stake the tent down in the middle of poison ivy, do you?"

Actually, I didn't want to stake the tent down anywhere at all. But now that I was a deacon, my father insisted I start doing more manly things. For starters, I had to watch at least one football game with him each week. I even had to learn the name of two prominent players, one from each of the teams competing that day, and one important statistic about each of those two players.

Of course, for as long as I could remember, I preferred sitting in my room reading Sir Arthur Conan Doyle or Edgar Allan Poe to watching men attack each other over a ball. I'd rather play Sudoku than take part in the Wave. Maybe listen to Handel or Pachelbel instead of the roar of the crowd. But Dad said over and over, "Classical music is for *asses*. Be a man."

So here we were at 4:30 on a Friday afternoon in early October. I was supposed to be studying for an American history test on Monday, but Dad had sprung this trip on me the second I got home from school.

I grabbed my backpack and followed him out the door. We listened to a biography of Steve Young as we drove past the Dairy Queen and Cash 'N Carry. We weren't driving to a park or campground, though, heading instead for Grandpa's three hundred acres outside of Brookhaven. This far south in Mississippi, it wasn't going to be cold over the weekend. Thank goodness for that. I just hoped it was cool enough to immobilize the snakes.

Dad stopped in front of Grandma and Grandpa's house and went inside to say hi while I stayed in the yard and played with their collie, who never got enough attention. I was impatient, though, wanting to get the tent up, eat a hamburger, and go to sleep.

The longer I could sleep, the less I'd have to endure. I was sure that escape was the main reason Heavenly Father had allowed the process of sleep to evolve in humans to begin with. With all the daily trials of Earth life, he had to give us at least a little break.

Though I don't suppose that explained why Mom liked to doze during Sacrament meeting.

If only she didn't wheeze when she slept. It was embarrassing.

Not that I wasn't tempted sometimes, too. I understood all about milk before meat, but if I already felt too old for most of the talks at the age of twelve, I couldn't imagine what it would be like listening to them at twenty, or thirty, or my parents' age.

There were times I simply didn't understand Heavenly Father very well, despite having read the New Testament and the Book of Mormon cover to cover. Sometimes, I thought…well, there was no point allowing myself to think anything negative about God. He could read minds. The only way to avoid letting him know what I really thought was not to think it.

When Dad came back to the car, we headed down a gravel pathway until we reached a fence. Dad pulled up on a loop of barbed wire to unhook a post and dragged back part of the fencing. We drove through, and Dad stopped to close the gap again.

We then drove through a pasture, around a bend, and down to the creek. There, Dad opened another gap so we could cross over the wooden bridge Grandpa had built when Dad was still a boy. Then we drove on a little farther, stopping at the tree line.

"We'll set up camp right here," my father announced.

Thank goodness he didn't plan on lugging the tent and our cooler through the woods. This weekend might not be so bad, after all. We soon had the tent set up with our sleeping bags laid out inside. Dad sprayed me and both the sleeping bags with Off and then had me spray him as well.

I was pleasantly surprised a few minutes later when Dad didn't ask me to start a fire but instead turned on a fake kerosene lamp, the kind with a light bulb and battery. Maybe it wasn't really Dad's goal to make me miserable. He honestly wanted to show me a good time. It wouldn't hurt me to make more of an effort.

Since Dad would hear all my secret thoughts on Judgment Day, I needed to avoid thinking anything bad about him, too.

"You don't mind cold hot dogs, do you, son?" he asked.

"Not at all." I smiled and opened the cooler. We sat on tiny fold out chairs with canvas seats—camp chairs, I supposed. Dad offered a solemn blessing on the food, and then we ate.

"I'll teach you everything you need to know," Dad promised. "You won't be a Tenderfoot for long. And you'll earn your Eagle before you turn fourteen."

The feeling of misery which had only just started to dissipate returned in an instant. How was one supposed to keep their mind free of bad thoughts when those thoughts were constantly being provoked? I remembered how happy I'd been a few months ago when I heard the Church announce it was discontinuing its association with the Boy Scouts.

Until I learned that scouting requirements were still in effect for twelve- and thirteen-year-olds. I considered a special fast to persuade Heavenly Father to cut ties altogether but then figured the Prophet must already know what he was doing. The day after the announcement, I'd passed by Dad's study and saw my mom on the computer laughing.

"What's so funny?" I asked.

"Nothing. Go do your homework."

I knew only men looked at porn on their computers, but Mom obviously wasn't the best Mormon. Several times, I'd heard her say something bad about the bishop. And I'd seen her more than once on the first Sunday of the month sneaking a spoonful of cottage cheese. So there was no telling what she might do.

As fortune would have it, though, the oven timer went off a moment later, and Mom took off for the kitchen. I snuck in to take a peek at the computer screen and frowned. It looked like a series of merit badges for the Church's revised scouting program.

What was there to laugh about, though? I'd always thought Mom was on my side, but the next two years promised nothing but hour after hour of discomfort. Did Mom just want me out of the house so she could pull out her racy romance novels? I'd once caught her reading *Fifty Shades of Gray*. I wasn't exactly sure what it was about, but I knew it was bad. Right and wrong meant black and white.

Peering at the computer screen, I saw one merit badge labeled First Aid, with a picture of the kind of key chain my father had, with a vial of consecrated oil on it. That was odd. Another badge was labeled Translating and featured what looked like a man throwing up into a hat.

I didn't get it.

Still another badge was named Blood Atonement and had an image of a bloody knife.

What the heck was Blood Atonement?

Mom had a weird sense of humor, that was for sure. I hoped she made it to the Celestial Kingdom with the rest of us. Though I had to admit, I often didn't feel very Celestial myself. Especially when I was watching football games.

"Do I really need to become an Eagle?" I asked Dad, taking another bite of my hot dog. "Normally, you have an extra two years to do the Eagle."

"If the Lord still wants deacons to be scouts, then he wants deacons to be Eagles."

Cold hot dogs didn't taste as good as I'd hoped, and the trip had only just begun. Since church didn't begin until 11:00 Sunday morning, we'd have no reason to come home Saturday night. I'd have to spend two nights outdoors. Dad started out the evening by telling me stories about bobcats and bears.

I knew he was trying to worry me, but I also knew the chances of seeing either of them out here were pretty slim. I was much more concerned about water moccasins and ticks. It didn't help that Dad decided we should go on a short hike right after sundown "to get this trip started off on the right foot."

Dad grabbed a huge Tactical flashlight and gave me one as well. He led the way through the trees, and within only a minute or so, I no longer had any idea which was the way back to the campsite. I hoped he wouldn't deliberately try to leave me behind as a test. He'd fiddled with the lawn mower this summer so it wouldn't start, expecting me to figure out how to fix it. He'd taken me to Home Depot once and expected me to pick out the kind of nails he needed for some project he was doing, as if I should somehow know simply because I was related to him.

At school, the teachers didn't test you until *after* they'd taught you what you needed to know.

But then, Heavenly Father always expected us to obey him before we had any real reason to. Laman and Lemuel were damned without ever having had a special witness of their father's ability to speak for the Lord.

"Look," said Dad, shining his light on the ground off to our right. "Deer spoor." He shone the light up at his face. It reminded me of the lighting in a horror movie I'd seen once. "That means predators won't be far away."

What it probably meant, I thought, was that the deer around here had no predators at all, but I could sense that the appropriate response was to look scared, so I complied.

Just the way my mom did all the time. I heard her complaining to our neighbor about Dad paying too much tithing. She complained to her sister, who'd married a Southern Baptist, about having to clean the ward meetinghouse once a month. She complained to the mail carrier, a young woman, about not being able to wear sleeveless dresses in the summer. But she didn't complain to Dad. She always looked a little scared around him.

"Think you can lead us back to camp, Hank?" my dad asked, shining his flashlight at me now.

I turned around and tried to make my way back, but after only a couple of minutes, Dad pushed me out of the way and directed the rest of our hike. I didn't see how he could tell one tree from another. I hated knowing I was going to disappoint my father yet again. And since scouting was an obligatory Church program, I supposed I was disappointing God as well.

I sure wished I could go to sleep.

I'd always thought people in comas were terribly unfortunate, but for the first time, I began to wonder if they weren't very lucky instead.

I was never so glad to see a fake kerosene lantern. Even with all the bugs flying around it.

"Do you think we got any ticks?" I asked as we sat back down.

"Take off your clothes and I'll inspect you." He grinned. "And I'll take off my clothes and you can inspect me."

I truly was worried about Lyme disease and who knew what else, so I did consider his suggestion for a long moment, but then I declined the offer. I hadn't seen my dad naked since the day of my baptism four years earlier, when we both changed clothes in the men's bathroom at church after he pushed me under the water. He had odd little scars on his chest which had frightened me.

It was a clear night, and I saw a couple of meteors. Dad talked about taking me to the shooting range to teach me how to use a rifle. He talked about taking me to the slaughterhouse so I could see the way meat was prepared. He talked about taking me canoeing one weekend in the spring when the water was high.

I wondered if I should try mocking my dad. If I was lucky, maybe there *would* be a bear tonight. A hungry she-bear.

Finally, when it seemed it must be well past midnight, Dad looked at his watch. "9:00," he said. "Time to hit the hay."

Despite my worries, I fell asleep almost instantly. I dreamed of Lamanites walking through these woods centuries ago. I dreamed of Mom at home renting R-rated Netflix movies while Dad and I were gone. I dreamed of going far away to college when I grew up. Maybe BYU where everyone was both nice and good.

When I awoke and stuck my head out of the tent, the first thing I saw was my father peeing on an ant hill. I realized I needed to relieve my bladder as well, but at least I made the effort to go behind a tree. There was no reason to behave like animals, after all.

Dad offered me some cheese and cold crackers for breakfast, and I ate them with vigor. The longer I ate, the less time there'd be for other activities. Dad finally had to take the box of crackers from me. "Don't spoil your appetite," he said. "We're having fish for lunch."

"Fish?"

"I brought poles so we could catch something in the creek."

"Maybe I'll just watch," I said. "I don't really want to clean any fish."

"No fish, no lunch."

I could live with that.

We walked across the pasture and sat on the wooden bridge. Better than fishing from the embankment, where there were worms and centipedes. Dad threw his line in the water, and we sat in the sun for an hour. Then two. Then three. Since there was a slight autumn chill, it wasn't too bad.

Except for the conversation. "Recite the twelve Articles of Faith," Dad demanded.

I did so.

"Tell me how the brother of Jared made light for the barges."

I told him about the rocks.

"Tell me what happened at Haun's Mill."

I recited the carnage that had taken place.

It wasn't as if any of the questions were hard. I studied the scriptures and Church history as much as my school subjects. I liked learning about stuff. Well, non-sports stuff. And in general I didn't even mind tests that much. The other kids in school thought I was trying to be the teacher's pet.

I had to admit, though, sometimes it felt as if Heavenly Father asked too much. At school, I could achieve whatever was asked of me. But at church, nothing I did was ever enough. I thought I understood Mom's temptation to fudge on the commandments a little. Was it *really* a sin to watch television on the Sabbath?

Darn it, I thought. Heavenly Father was going to know I thought that.

I decided I didn't like being tested every second of the day while already having to endure this outing, and by the time Dad finally caught a fish, I was grateful for the distraction.

"One fish isn't enough for a meal," Dad said, ripping the hook out of the fish's mouth. "I'll let it go."

I suspected he didn't want to clean fish, either.

We walked along the edge of the woods on our way back to camp and stopped when we came across some blackberry bushes. Most of the good berries were long since gone, but there were a few left we could eat.

A very few. And half dried out. Dad picked at a few berries on other bushes, but I didn't recognize them and decided not to follow his example.

I made a point of not saying anything about food when we sat back down at the campsite. About ten minutes later, Dad reached in the cooler and pulled out a can of peaches. He handed it to me and then grabbed a can for himself. I wolfed down the fruit and drank every last drop of the syrup as well.

"Tell me about Carthage," Dad said.

I recounted the martyrdom of Joseph Smith.

"Tell me about the trek across the plains."

This was scouting, I wondered? This was the worst of both worlds. I was grateful when Dad suggested we take a hike through the woods a little later. Because we were in single file, we didn't even have to talk that much. I heard something rustle in the bushes off to our left but didn't say anything since Dad didn't. I saw a small skull and a few other bones but didn't say anything about that, either, since Dad didn't. I saw an empty pack of chewing tobacco among some leaves and didn't say anything.

I hoped there were no hunters trespassing today.

Around 2:30, the moment I'd been dreading since this whole trip started finally arrived. "Dad," I said, "I have to go to the bathroom."

"There's a tree, Hank." Dad pointed. "Go behind it and pee like a man."

"I don't have to pee," I clarified. I felt my cheeks burning and wanted to sink right into the ground.

Dad laughed, making everything worse. "That's part of life in the wild outdoors," he said. "Look, see that bush over there?"

"Yes."

"You can use those leaves to wipe yourself. I'll go stand over behind that big tree till you're done."

I nodded and waited for my dad to disappear before I walked over to the bush and squatted down. I'd forced myself to go to the bathroom yesterday before we left home, hoping I could hold off needing to defecate again until we went back home on Sunday.

I hadn't even made it a full day.

I did my business as quickly as I could, grateful for a hard stool, and wiped myself with the leaves Dad had indicated. It was a strange sensation, rough and wet, but I finished and pulled up my pants. Hopefully, I wouldn't have to do that again until I was back in civilization as God intended.

Assuming God ever intended things which made life easier.

As we continued our hike, I eventually became convinced Dad was just leading me around in a circle. Even three hundred acres wasn't enough to keep us going this long. When we came upon a beehive with bees flying dangerously close by, I finally spoke up. "Let's go back to camp, Dad."

"What's this really called, Hank?" He pointed.

"Deseret."

Dad nodded. "We can head back now."

Over the past couple of hours, as the hike dragged on, I'd begun feeling more and more uncomfortable. Before we reached the campsite, my butt was itching terribly and burning just a little, too. I held off as long as I could, but I finally began scratching myself. Somehow, that only made things worse. After one particularly vigorous scratch, Dad laughed.

"What?" I said.

"Hank, you really should have studied the scouting handbook I gave you last week."

"Why?"

"Then you'd have known the leaves I told you to use were poison ivy." He laughed again.

I stopped in my tracks. Had I heard right? I scratched myself again. The itch was maddening, but the more I scratched, the more my butt burned.

"You're mean," I said. What if I'd rubbed my eyes after handling the leaves?

"You gonna believe anything someone tells you just because they're in charge?" he countered. "I'm teaching you a lesson that will serve you well in life. This whole weekend is about lessons."

"We need to go back to the house," I said, trying to keep my voice calm. "I'm dying."

Dad laughed yet again. "You'll remember what those leaves look like now, won't you?" I didn't reply and he shrugged. "I have some calamine lotion back at the camp."

I carefully read every word on the label before opening the bottle. The lotion helped, but I was still miserable. It made paying attention to the knot-tying lesson Dad gave next rather difficult. I'd thought I was tired of the religious instruction, but now I remembered why I hadn't wanted to come camping in the first place. Thinking of tying my dad to a tree overnight kept up my interest a little, but even that fantasy soon lost its appeal.

Especially since I was now distracted by the chigger bites I'd incurred throughout the day. They itched almost as much as the poison ivy. Dad stopped his lesson to hand me a Sprite and a can of beans. "Maybe if you fart a lot, it'll help your ass," he said, laughing.

I took the can and ate in silence.

Did Dad really expect me to go on campouts like this for a whole two years? Did Heavenly Father? I wondered if I could talk my folks *and* Heavenly Father into sending me to boarding school until I turned fourteen. There was one down on the coast in Bay St. Louis. It was a Catholic school, but maybe it would be good to get away from Mormonism for a while.

Mom was setting such a bad example. I was *not* going to sneak cottage cheese on Fast Sunday.

The sun finally set, and I could feel time moving ahead ever so slowly. Sitting by the lantern, I kept swatting at mosquitoes as Dad talked about hunting deer with his father. "The bug spray isn't working very well," I interrupted.

I wondered if he'd replaced the liquid in the Off bottle with something that attracted bugs instead. Another lesson. That would explain the chigger bites, too. But he didn't seem affected by the insects, and he'd used the same stuff.

"You need to respect mosquitoes," Dad said. "They're going to the Celestial Kingdom."

"Excuse me?" I slapped my face again.

"They fill the measure of their creation," Dad continued. "That's more than I can say for you. You're supposed to be tough, and all you do is complain."

My face now felt as warm as my butt. Dad was right, of course. I realized to my shame I really was being a wuss. I didn't want to be the kind of person who whined every time things got a little difficult. I hated the kids at school who had bad attitudes. The kids who always asked, "Is this going to be on the test?" rather than just learning things because it was good to learn.

"I guess poison ivy fills the measure of its creation, too," I said.

Dad laughed. "Yep."

Finally, it was time for bed, and I recognized that my newfound positive attitude hadn't even lasted two hours. I still wanted to sleep away the rest of the trip until it was time to go home. But my butt was driving me crazy. I'd never be able to relax. I hadn't complained since my dad's judgment, but I did still fidget on my chair. "Here." Dad handed me some capsules. "I knew this would happen, so I brought some sleeping pills."

It felt like the first nice thing he'd done for me all weekend, but then I remembered I wouldn't need the pills in the first place if it weren't for him. Wasn't that kind of like Heavenly Father giving us the priesthood after giving us a world full of disease?

"Thank you." I swallowed the capsules and slid into my sleeping bag, still fully clothed except for my shoes. But I lay awake for a long time, wondering how I was going to survive the next six years until I left on my mission.

I slept fitfully even with the sleeping aid, dreaming of fire ants and chiggers and ticks. I even had a dream I was being strapped to an electric chair. I'd have to stop reading articles about capital punishment, even if the extra reading did help me in history class. But finally, after a long, unpleasant night, I woke up when I felt something pricking my right leg just above the knee.

Oh, my heck, I thought. A water moccasin must have gotten into my sleeping bag!

I opened my eyes in terror, squinting immediately at the bright sunlight. It was well past dawn. I must've slept late. But wait, I thought, why wasn't I still in the shade of the tent? I tried to shield my eyes but found I couldn't move my hands. What the—

As my eyes adjusted, I was slowly able to focus on my dad standing above me. He was holding a knife in his hands, raised over me like he was going to stab me. Was I still dreaming? "Dad?" What was going on?

"Good morning, son." He sounded so calm.

"Dad?" I repeated. Why couldn't I move? Had I been bitten by something that paralyzed me? Was it still here, about to attack me again? Maybe that was what Dad was about to stab with the knife.

"You remember the story of Abraham sacrificing Isaac." It wasn't a question.

"Y-yes?" I lifted my head and saw to my horror that I was completely tied up and staked to the ground. I was naked except for my underwear.

"Heavenly Father has let me know I must sacrifice you," he said. "The scouting trip was just to get you out here." He laughed. "And you fell for it." He stopped smiling. "Everyone fell for it."

"Dad—" Maybe he'd eaten a poison berry yesterday and was going crazy. The knife was still poised over me. I could see a tiny red spot on my leg where Dad had already pricked me with the knife to wake me up.

I remembered asking Mom once about a bruise on her arm and her covering it up quickly as if she were embarrassed.

"Now, Hank," Dad said, "this sacrifice will only bless *me* if *you're* willing to obey Heavenly Father, too. I know your testimony is still weak. You're too influenced by your mother, but you wouldn't want to miss out on a blessing, would you?"

He brought the knife down to my chest and cut me again, this time under my right nipple. I could see a few drops of blood pooling on my skin. "You wouldn't want to die in vain." He cut a spot under my left nipple. He cut a tiny spot near my navel.

My heart was beating so violently I could feel it pounding against my chest as if trying to break out of my rib cage. But I couldn't raise my arm to the square and command my father to drop the knife. I couldn't hit him. I couldn't kick him. I couldn't dodge out of his way.

"Dad," I said as calmly as I could, "Heavenly Father appeared to *me* in a dream last night and told me to tell you Satan put that idea in your head. You are *not* supposed to sacrifice me."

Why couldn't I think of a story from the scriptures that would back up my lie? All I could think about was Nephi chopping off Laban's head. All I could think of was Shiz getting his head cut off.

"Son, I always obey the Lord." He raised the knife a little higher. "Tell me you're willing, Hank."

Suddenly, another six years with this man seemed too much. Another sixty years with this God, who had assigned me to my father in the Pre-Existence. I was not willing to spend eternity with either of them.

"I'm willing," I lied again. Maybe I was still feeling tired from the sleeping pills, but I just wanted it all over with. "Do it, Dad."

I saw the knife rushing down toward me and closed my eyes, but instead of feeling a piercing stab to my chest, I heard a piercing cry. "You did it, Hank! You did it!"

I opened my eyes and looked up at my father, who was smiling down at me. Was this another of his stupid lessons?

I hated him.

"You'll be an Eagle for sure," he said. "And you'll be Seminary class president in high school. And a zone leader on your mission. Hank…" My father put the knife down and wiped his eyes. "You've made me very proud."

"Thank you, Dad," I said calmly, "for teaching me a lesson." I smiled up at him. I hoped it looked sincere. "Can you untie me now?"

As he worked on the knots, I kept my eyes on the knife. I wanted to stab him, maybe pin his hand to the top of the cooler, maybe pin his foot to the ground. I could probably figure out how to drive the car back to the house by myself. If only Dad couldn't unpin himself so easily.

"Here." Dad dabbed my chest with a cloth and pulled out a box of bandages. "I can teach you some First Aid."

I thought of the merit badges my mom had been looking at.

As my dad taped up the last of the wounds, I found myself hoping a trespassing hunter would come out of the woods, after all. I could yell I was being attacked by a deranged man, and the hunter would shoot him.

I wondered why a she-bear hadn't come out and killed my dad when he was mocking me yesterday.

"There now. You're all better." Dad put the box of bandages away and clapped me on the shoulder. "I was twelve when my father took me on a camping trip like this." He chuckled and shook his head. "We've been close ever since."

He held up two fingers, crossed like he was making a wish. Then he reached for the cooler. "How about some cold Jimmy Dean sausage for breakfast?" he asked. "Then we'll go home and get ready for church."

I nodded and held out my hand.

Faith-Promoting Faith

"Wh...w...wh...where's…Ca...Cathy?" Clara's eyebrows furrowed. Douglas fluffed the pillow behind her and helped her ease back into it.

"Cathy said she couldn't come," Douglas replied. Cathy was one of Clara's friends from Relief Society. Whenever the woman called to speak with Clara, Douglas told her she was in the shower. "She had something she needed to do with her daughter."

"I...I...I...w...want...L...Laura."

"Oh, honey," Douglas said soothingly, "you remember. I told you she's busy with Visiting Teaching. She has to take over your assignments, too, these days."

Clara nodded and closed her eyes.

"You rest, dear." Douglas leaned down and kissed his wife on the forehead. She'd come a long way since her stroke two months earlier, but her progress seemed to have slowed considerably after an early rebound. While she wasn't paralyzed, she still showed significant weakness on her right side, still had trouble walking, still had problems with her memory. She was speaking more clearly now but still couldn't seem to recognize letters and numbers.

Douglas dimmed the bedroom light and pressed Play on the CD player. The Mormon Tabernacle Choir started singing "God Rest Ye Merry Gentlemen." It wasn't Christmastime, but Clara seemed to like holiday music best, and thinking about the Savior was sure to help in her recovery.

He closed the door softly before heading downstairs. He turned the TV on low so he could hear Clara if she called for anything. *NCIS: New Orleans* was one of his favorite shows. He and Clara had visited the city several times back when she was still fun to be with. It was close enough to their home in Houston that they could drive. Clara had always hated flying, had absolutely refused to do so the past few years. It seemed he was always accommodating her needs lately, when she was supposed to be following his lead.

During a pivotal moment in the show, Douglas heard the tinkling of a bell and sighed. It was too bad he couldn't hire nursing assistants around the clock. The two daytime caregivers were already costing him plenty, even with the help of insurance, and it wouldn't be right not to make an effort to do some of the work himself. During the next commercial break, he headed upstairs.

"You need something, sweetheart?"

"B...b...bath...bath..."

"Sure thing, honey." Douglas pulled down the covers and helped swing Clara's legs off the bed and to the floor. She grabbed onto his arm, but he knew she wouldn't be able to steady herself alone. He held her firmly and guided her slowly to the en suite bathroom. She only wore the top half of her garments since coming home, to make it easier getting on and off the toilet.

"W...w...walk...walker." Clara breathed heavily. "C...c...can walk...with...w...walk...walker."

She'd asked Douglas to buy her a walker several times, but she seemed to keep forgetting his answer. Not a good sign. "You're going to be better in no time," he said soothingly. "There's no need for a walker."

After helping Clara back to bed, Douglas hurried downstairs, but he'd missed the end of his show. Dagnabbit. Oh, well, the Lord required sacrifice from everyone, didn't he? That was part of life. Clara had always been a good wife, did everything she was supposed to do. Until the last few years, when she'd started going to movies by herself.

She also attended some author lectures without him. She took an online poetry workshop, though she couldn't write anything that rhymed to save her life. She'd even driven to San Antonio by herself one time and stayed the entire weekend. Didn't even call.

Douglas had almost expected the stroke. To be sure, Heavenly Father didn't always punish women when they started to drift away from their husbands. Douglas certainly saw that at work every day. And he wasn't positive Clara's stroke was entirely her fault or if some of the blame might be his own. After all, he was the one who'd failed to keep her committed to him. Perhaps this current crisis was all to bring Douglas back in line as much as it was Clara.

How he despised thinking he might be the one at fault. He'd considered not partaking of the sacrament one week, but what would people think? Besides, it did no good to brood. Not while the bread and water were being passed, and not now. Fortunately, an episode of *Diagnosis: Murder* had just started on one of the oldie channels. After working all day at the law firm and caring for his wife all evening, he deserved some time to relax.

At a crucial point in the show, however, Douglas heard Clara tinkling her bell. He sighed again and headed upstairs, even before the commercial break. "You okay, sweetie?"

"O…O...J...OJ."

"Darling, you know you can't have too much sugar. There's water right on the bedside table. Here, let me get you some." He poured it into her sippy cup and secured the lid. He didn't really expect her to get it herself, but it just seemed mean not to have it within reaching distance in case he fell asleep on the sofa downstairs or got caught on the phone discussing BYU football with a friend.

Douglas hurried back to the television to watch the last few minutes of his show and then poured himself a small glass of apple juice and headed up the stairs once more. He brushed his teeth and walked over to the bed.

"Need anything before I turn out the light?"

"N..no."

Douglas smiled and pulled off the bottom half of his garments. He turned off the light and slid under the covers next to Clara. He leaned over to kiss her, and she moaned. That sound always got his motor running. He put his hand on her right breast and squeezed softly.

"P...p...please..."

"Of course, sweetheart. Of course I will. I still find you attractive. You know that." Motab was still singing softly from the other side of the room.

"P...p...please..."

He put his lips on hers again. Heaven knew they both needed something pleasant in their lives these days. Douglas caressed Clara's stomach a moment and then reached down to gently pry open her legs.

In the morning, Douglas heated a bowl of oatmeal, sprinkling it liberally with brown sugar and raisins, gobbling it down quickly before going back upstairs to brush his teeth and check on Clara one last time before heading to work.

"P...po...poach...poached...eggs?" she asked.

"I've got to run," Douglas replied, "but the nurse will be here in a few minutes. She can fix you something." He leaned down to kiss her and headed back down the stairs. Douglas had hired two immigrants to help with Clara on alternating days. One of the young women was from Somalia and the other from El Salvador. He'd had them both sign Non-Disclosure Agreements before he let them anywhere near Clara.

It was all he could do to keep the ward members from knowing her true condition, and he didn't want the nurses blabbing to anyone, not even their ethnic friends. When he'd given her a blessing two months earlier with the assistance of his Home Teaching companion, Clara had made remarkable progress in just a few days. The doctor hadn't even thought she'd regain consciousness. It was a true miracle.

The Relief Society sisters had visited the hospital daily those first couple of weeks, had brought food to the house for another week after Clara was released, as much to support Douglas as Clara. Jerri and Wayne, his and Clara's two adult children, had called from Virginia and California to speak to her on the phone two successive Sundays, as awkward as that had been. But then the progress had stopped, and that's when Douglas knew he still hadn't passed the trial of his faith.

"Good morning, Mr. Montgomery," the receptionist said when Douglas strode into the office. She was matronly, just the right type of woman for a work environment. "How's everything?"

He smiled, his lips parting just enough to reveal a thin line of ivory teeth. "We're fine." He thought of Clara and himself as a unit and never replied to questions like this in the singular. "Thanks for asking, hon."

He continued on to his private office and got started on the day's work. As a divorce attorney, he saw the consequences of Satan's machinations every day. One of the cases he was working on currently involved a woman who'd come out as a lesbian at the age of forty.

Good grief. What was she thinking? Another case concerned a woman who'd sold all her husband's comic books behind his back. In other cases, a husband had cheated with a coworker, a wife had treated her husband with emotional neglect, another husband had committed spousal rape. Such repulsive behavior. It was so hard upon meeting his clients not to offer them lessons on gospel principles. The Church could solve so many of the world's problems, if only HR would allow it.

And if one had enough faith. Douglas wasn't sure why his faith hadn't been sufficient to heal his wife. So truly puzzling. He'd always done everything he was supposed to. A mission. A temple marriage. Scripture study. Church attendance. Tithing. Raising two good kids. Though Clara had handled that last one by herself for the most part. Still, he'd always set the example, and that was half the battle.

Where had he failed?

Obviously, he couldn't let the bishop or anyone else know of Clara's continued limitations. At best, one could achieve only the tiniest of victories in this life. Even when he was a "success" at work, it only meant he'd helped break up families. There was so little to cling to in the Last Days. Clara's stroke *had* to be faith-promoting, whether he had the requisite faith or not. The least he could do was assist others in finding faith through his personal triumph.

That was the single most challenging issue with the Book of Mormon. It ended with everyone in apostasy. Sure, there was the inspiring promise that after the restoration of the gospel many hundreds of years later, the Lamanites would finally discover their faith. But it hadn't happened yet, and Douglas could only bask in the happy ending if he pretended it was more than theoretical. A non-happy happy ending just felt empty.

It wasn't enough that the other members of the congregation believed he and Clara were eventually going to prove themselves faithful. It had to be true *now* to have any real effect. And it could only be true if they didn't know the truth.

Just after 12:00, the receptionist forwarded a call from the day nurse to Douglas's desk. "What's up, Bishaaro?" he asked. It was the Somali's shift today.

"Mr. Montgomery," she replied in a heavy accent, "your wife wants me to call her friend Jeanette, but I know you told me not to."

Jeanette Miller was the Relief Society president. "Tell Clara you called and left a message, but that Sister Miller wasn't home."

"Yes, Mr. Montgomery."

"Thanks for checking with me, Bishaaro." Douglas had made it clear at the start that if the nurses didn't respect his authority, he'd have to let them go. "Remember that I'm the one paying you, not my wife," he'd told them.

The women watched TV in the bedroom with Clara, prepared simple meals, helped her to the bathroom, bathed her, encouraged her to talk. They did everything any of the Relief Society sisters could, except judge.

And it didn't matter if the nurses' faith grew stronger or not.

Each Sunday at church for the past few weeks, Douglas answered inquiries by saying Clara was recovering on schedule but was still a little too tired to return to services. Admitting even that much defeat was embarrassing.

Confessing that Clara needed to rest already implied some weakness of character, but it was simply the best he could do.

Douglas was sure the steady devotion he showed to her welfare, though, would eventually sway Heavenly Father to honor the priesthood blessing he'd sealed upon his wife. He'd read Spencer W. Kimball's *Faith Precedes the Miracle* as a teen. He knew how these things worked.

The last book Clara had read before her stroke was *A Head for Business*. She wanted to make and sell jewelry.

Please. She'd never even been able to help the kids when they tried to sell lemonade on the sidewalk, back in the prime of her life.

Women could be so much happier if they just stopped kicking against the pricks. Since the stroke, Clara hadn't mentioned any of her excursions of the last few years. Perhaps Heavenly Father had wiped the slate clean, and she was ready to start obeying her temple covenants again.

Douglas tried to wipe his own mind clean and concentrate on his cases for the rest of the afternoon. The woman who'd sold her husband's comic books had also bought herself an upgraded wedding ring with the money. It would be laughable if it weren't so tragic.

On the way home from the office, Douglas picked up some fried rice. Clara loved it so, and she deserved a treat once in a while. She could sometimes say "Tabernacle" in one breath these days. Though still not consistently. He bought some General Tso chicken for himself.

Then, up in the bedroom, he set a tray on Clara's lap, watching as she grabbed the fork awkwardly with her left hand. He opened his box in the stuffed chair a few feet away and ate slowly. He didn't want to finish too far ahead of her. It would only remind her how much work she still had ahead. One had to be sensitive about these things.

"Did you do your therapy today?"

She nodded. "G...g...go...ch...church...s...soon?"

"I'm sure it won't be long."

"C...call...Cath...Cathy…?"

"I'll call her again after dinner, sweetheart. You're doing so well. Such a brave girl."

Clara asked in her maddening manner if she could talk to Jerri in Virginia, but Douglas assured her their daughter was planning to visit shortly and they could catch up then. Clara's memory was clearly not back to normal yet, as she kept asking the same question almost every day.

Douglas was keeping the two kids at bay by explaining their mother wanted to grow a little stronger before talking to them again. When they called anyway, he simply said their mother was napping. But he couldn't keep this up forever. He had to develop more faith. Clara needed to be healed.

"L...lap...laptop?"

"I'm still not sure that's a good idea. You were always clicking on links that infected us with viruses even before the stroke, and your judgment has been off even more since then, so—"

"Y...you...c...could...w...watch..."

Douglas smiled. The woman couldn't even read anymore. What was the point? He leaned over to wipe the corner of Clara's mouth. "Sure, honey, I'll think about it. I promise."

After they finished eating, Clara asked if Douglas would sit with her so they could watch TV together. The problem was that after the stroke she only seemed to like sitcoms, and that type of show bored him to tears. Even worse were her occasional attempts to suggest the "H...H...Hallmark" channel or, God forbid, "L...L...Lifetime."

Her eyes bore into his now. "H...H..." she began.

"I have some work to do in the office downstairs," Douglas replied, "but I'll keep the door open so I can hear the bell." He moved the remote from the bedside table to the dresser and turned on the CD player. "Silent Night" drifted softly through the room.

Douglas took the Chinese food containers down to the kitchen so the nurse could dispose of them in the morning and then turned the television on low in the living room. A great episode of *Law and Order* was on tonight. Since he already knew the ending, it wasn't a big deal to go back upstairs when he heard Clara's bell tinkling.

But he began wondering about the timing. Was she deliberately trying to interrupt him at the most important point of every program?

Well, he just had to be patient, didn't he? The poor thing needed to vent her frustrations over Heavenly Father's reticence somehow. Husbands who truly loved their wives put up with these things with a smile as they guided them lovingly toward a healthier response.

"O...O...OJ?"

Douglas poured some water into Clara's sippy cup, gave her an affectionate kiss on the forehead, and returned to the living room. After his show was over, he put his feet up on the coffee table and read a little further in *The Runaway Jury*, a book he'd started for a third reading two weeks ago. It was his favorite John Grisham novel, so triumphant in combatting the evil tobacco industry.

The movie version wasn't worth seeing, liberals in Hollywood making the trial about gun control instead. Sometimes, reading or watching legal dramas could get annoying even at the best of times, since it was so easy to see the inaccuracies. But Douglas always felt a little thrill at realizing again and again how much more he knew than the rest of the public.

One more trip upstairs to help Clara pee, and then back down to work on his lesson for the High Priests group on Sunday. Of course, the topic absolutely had to be faith. It had become abundantly clear that everyone needed to focus on it all the time. If *he* lacked sufficient faith after the dedicated life he'd lived, the other high priests in the ward certainly did, too.

Maybe it was *Clara's* lack of faith that prevented her from a full recovery. It might not be his fault at all. Perhaps he should practice his lesson on his wife first. They *both* needed to develop their faith if they wanted to be gods one day. There was no use making it to the Celestial Kingdom alone. Sure, he'd be given other wives up in the highest degree of heaven, but he loved Clara. He'd try his lesson out on her tomorrow after dinner.

Once he'd written down some questions to generate a good discussion in Priesthood meeting, Douglas poured himself a small glass of apple juice and then went upstairs to brush his teeth. He walked to the dresser and turned off the CD player in the middle of "I Heard the Bells on Christmas Day."

"You need anything, honey, before I turn out the light?"

Clara shook her head silently, staring at the ceiling. Looking heavenward the way everyone should. Learning to be righteous even in the midst of suffering. Douglas grinned and tugged off the bottom half of his garments. He climbed into bed and kissed Clara passionately on the lips. When he pulled back for a second to breathe, Clara moaned, "Oh...oh...D...Doug..."

"Oh, Clara!" he returned breathlessly. He'd always liked sex more than she did, but now that physical love was the only thing she could contribute to the marriage, she was really making an effort. An incredible woman. He reached down and gently spread her legs before crawling on top of her. When he was finished, he whispered in her ear. "I love you, sweetheart."

He saw a tear paused high on her cheek and felt deeply touched. He watched in fascination as gravity finally pulled it down, like dew on a morning bloom. "I thought making love with you was beautiful, too," he said softly, his heart swelling.

It was almost certain they were going to get through this. They were passing the trial of their faith. One day, he'd give a talk about Clara's stroke in stake conference. He might finally be called to the stake presidency himself.

He let out a contented sigh and rolled over, feeling the warmth of the Holy Ghost resonating in his chest.

Grandma Is a Slutty Perv

"Mr. Robinson, this session will be filmed and recorded, but I may take notes as well." The police psychologist tapped her notebook and looked at me in a not unfriendly way, even if she didn't smile. She was about forty, with short, strawberry blond hair, and skin that showed she spent far too much time outdoors for someone with her natural lack of melanin.

"Call me Noel, Dr. Plath," I said. I looked at the large mirror on the wall behind her, noting my prominent Adam's apple. I smiled at the people I knew were behind the glass. I was used to being watched.

"Noel." Dr. Plath gave a short nod to acknowledge my request. Her hair was too short to brush behind her ear but she made a casual swipe as if she thought her hair was longer. "Can you tell me how all this started? How long this has been going on?"

"Well," I said, "I'm twenty-two now, and I must have taken the first step back when I was a kid in Primary."

"Primary?"

"It's a children's organization for Mormons," I explained. "I remember one of my teachers talking to us about the Spirit World."

"Spirit World?"

"It's a combination of both Spirit Prison and Paradise," I went on. "Spirit Prison is for all the bad people who've died. It's where they go while waiting for Judgment Day. Paradise is where the mostly decent spirits wait."

I frowned as I watched Dr. Plath scribble something down. "It's not a clear distinction, though," I continued. "I think sometimes even good spirits go to Spirit Prison if they weren't Mormon while on Earth." I rubbed my chin.

"But that would make the per capita incarceration rate in the afterlife even higher than what we have here in the U.S.," I said, "so I don't really know for sure how it all works." Incarceration, I thought. I might as well get used to the idea, both on Earth and in the world to come.

"How did your teacher talking about the...Spirit World...lead to your problem?"

I shrugged. "I think it was because she said the Spirit World was right here on Earth. Kind of like a different dimension occupying the same space. Only the spirits could see us all the time, even if we couldn't see them."

Dr. Plath held up a hand. "Your teacher told you there were ghosts all around you?"

"Not ghosts. Spirits. I asked my mom when I got home, and she told me the same thing. Our dead ancestors were watching us every minute, trying to offer invisible encouragement to keep us from sinning."

"Doesn't seem to have worked," Dr. Plath said, her lips pressed together. "So what went wrong?"

"Well, it creeped me out. My mom said these spirits could see every moment if we'd been bad or good."

Dr. Plath looked as if she was going to ask a clarifying question, but she remained silent and let me go on.

"I asked my dad if it was kind of like Santa. He said Santa is fake but that myth of surveillance comes from the deeper knowledge of the way the universe actually works." I paused for a long moment. "Do you know the song by Rockwell? 'Somebody's Watching Me'?"

"I'm not familiar with that one."

"You should YouTube it."

Dr. Plath looked at her watch. "Noel, I don't see where this is going."

"At first, I was ashamed to go to the bathroom anymore. What else did a kid have to feel embarrassed about? My cousin Diana was killed in a car accident when she was seven. Was she watching me pee? My grandpa—my mom's father—died of a heart attack a few months earlier. Was he watching me poop? I got to where I was holding it all in as long as possible, trying to do my business after dark, with the lights out. I didn't figure spirits had night vision goggles." I grimaced and held up both hands with my fingers crossed.

"Noel," Dr. Plath said calmly, "you were not arrested for urinating in the dark."

"I know, I know." I stared at the table for a moment, wishing I could die and move on to the Spirit World myself. At least in Spirit Prison, I wouldn't be haunted by unseen eyes anymore. I looked into the mirror on the wall behind Dr.

Plath and fought an urge to stick up my middle finger. "I need to be put away," I said. "But I don't know if prison or a mental institution is best. I obviously need counseling if I'm ever going to get better. But I don't know if I'll be able to plead Not Guilty by Reason of Insanity. I'm not really crazy, after all. I just need a little therapy."

I didn't understand how people starred in reality shows like *Big Brother*, where every move was monitored for the whole world to see. How many of those contestants ended up in counseling after their season ended?

"That's partly what I'm here to determine." Dr. Plath again gave me that almost friendly expression which still lacked a smile.

I nodded, afraid to smile myself in case she interpreted that as a sexual advance. "So anyway," I continued, "I ended up constipated a lot and a little dehydrated, but I never needed any medical treatment for it. When I turned twelve, though, another of my cousins died. Dean was thirteen. He had a bowel obstruction."

"Did he...?" Dr. Plath asked. "Was he...?" She held up a hand. "Never mind. Go on."

"After that, I not only felt embarrassed about going to the bathroom but guilty, too. It seemed a slap in Dean's face for me to have a bowel movement when he couldn't. Sometimes, if it was hard enough, I tried to shove it back inside. I wanted to stop taking the sacrament on Sunday—you know, the bread and water to remind us of Christ's atonement—but I knew my parents would ask why, and I couldn't bear to tell them."

Dr. Plath jotted something down and circled it.

"My teachers noticed my grades slipping. They asked my parents what was wrong, and then my parents confronted me. I just said I missed Dean. After that, I worked harder in class so no one would ask any more questions."

Dr. Plath nodded.

"And then things went from embarrassing to mortifying." I took two or three deep breaths while Dr. Plath waited patiently. "I discovered masturbation." I shook my head. "If I felt ashamed having my relatives watch me urinate, you can imagine what it was like having them watch me abusing myself."

Dr. Plath murmured but didn't look at me as she scribbled something else in her notebook.

"And I didn't just beat off," I said. In times past, my face would have turned red to address any of this openly, but of course these days I could be explicit without shame.

But, of course, there was still plenty of shame, wasn't there? In fact, the shame had become the thrill, the driving force behind my actions. I knew I needed help.

Unfortunately, psychiatry could only do so much. What I needed was an exorcism. But how did one exorcise the entire Spirit World?

"Sometimes, I beat off into a gym sock. I beat off in the shower on a bar of soap and then rubbed the soap all over my body. I grabbed a piece of liver from the fridge, wrapped it around my dick, and beat off on it. Then I washed it and put it back in the refrigerator."

Dr. Plath stopped writing and gave me a penetrating stare.

"TMI?" I asked.

"I need to understand what's motivating you, Noel. You weren't arrested for masturbating on animal organs in the privacy of your home." She made it sound nasty. I felt a twitch in my groin but kept my face blank. "I need you to get to the behavior in question."

I sighed and gave her a nod. "The masturbation kept on throughout my teens," I said. "And I was doing it in lots of disgusting ways. I felt depraved for wanting any sexual release at all, so I made sure to *be* depraved. I wanted to make it easier for Heavenly Father to punish me."

Dr. Plath wrote something down.

"My mom's mother died right after I'd been ordained a priest."

Dr. Plath looked back up at me.

"I continued to feel mortified every time I beat off, but I couldn't stop myself. I fasted. I wrapped my groin in a thick bedsheet when I went to sleep. I hung up a poster of a dying cow on my bedroom wall so I could call up that image whenever I needed to lose my erection. I'd make it two or three days without, sometimes a week, but I always ended up whacking off again. I could feel Grandma and Grandpa watching me. I could feel Diana and Dean watching me. I could feel their disgust."

I put my hands on the table and stared at my fingernails. "Of course, it was nothing compared to the disgust I felt for myself. Whenever I looked in the mirror, I saw a tub of worms."

Dr. Plath turned her head and glanced backward at the mirror behind her.

"You know that song by the Police? 'Every Breath You Take'?"

Dr. Plath nodded.

"Every time I heard that song, I heard Diana's voice singing the lyrics. I heard Dean singing. I heard my grandma singing." I closed my eyes. "I started hearing them sing even when the song wasn't playing."

Dr. Plath froze, her pen paused over the notebook in her hand. "Do you often hear voices that aren't there?"

I slapped the table, and Dr. Plath jumped. I think I even scared myself. I took a couple of deep breaths and then held up both hands as if stopping traffic, to show I was back in control. "I finally began to get mad at all those spirits making my life miserable with their spying."

I smiled, though the subject wasn't humorous. "You know, live Mormons spy on each other all the time, too. Your Home Teachers report back on you. Your Visiting Teachers report back. Your roommates at BYU report back. They all blab to the bishop or other leaders."

I interpreted the look on Dr. Plath's face as disbelief. She thought I was being paranoid, I realized sadly. She didn't understand what life was like for Mormons.

"The idea that even in the Spirit World we had to keep up the spying became infuriating. One day while I was fapping, I looked around my bedroom and whispered, 'What's the *matter* with you, Grandma? Why are you watching me? Haven't you got better things to do? Are you some kind of sex fiend?'" I exhaled heavily. "And that's when things went from sin to abomination."

Dr. Plath scribbled away in her notebook furiously.

I thought it best not to tell her about the dozen or so times I ejaculated into the trash can in the sacrament closet behind the podium. Even as a priest, I often had to prepare the sacrament myself if no one from the Teacher's Quorum showed up. It was always easier to concentrate on the prayer cards later if I'd exorcised my penis first.

If only there were some way to cast the entirety of my sexuality out altogether. I wondered if that was why the spirits of my family kept watch so tenaciously. Without their mortal bodies, watching me was the closest they had to experiencing physical feelings of their own.

So who was the real sex addict here?

"I started trying to be disgusting on purpose," I said, "to force the spirits to leave me alone. I'll spare you the details, but trust me, most normal people would have turned away. After one particularly repulsive act, I felt sure I was finally free. But then..." I still remembered the devastating news.

Dr. Plath looked at me expectantly but said nothing.

"My mom told me the day after I received my mission call to Greece that she'd had a vivid dream during which her parents promised to watch over me every minute I was away." I put my hands on the table and shook my head, still recalling the mixture of misery and resignation I'd felt over the revelation.

"Every minute for the next two years," I said. "There was no escape from Grandma and Grandpa. No escape at all." I let out a mirthless laugh. "Mom thought she was comforting me, but she'd just cursed me instead. There was really no hope for a normal life after that."

Dr. Plath frowned and tapped her pen against her chin. "Let me get this straight, Noel," she said carefully. "If your mother's parents were watching you, who was watching her? Why did you think *you* were so special?"

I slapped the table again. "That's just it! The spirits watch *everyone* they ever knew who is still alive. They're like the Holy Ghost—they're everywhere!" I could hear my voice tremble. "Everywhere."

"Like God." Dr. Plath jotted it down in her notebook. "Omnipresent."

"But that's only because they're spirits," I said. "God isn't really everywhere at once. He has a physical body and so can only be in one place at a time, but the Holy Ghost is a spirit and can be everywhere." I held my head in my hands. "None of it makes any sense, does it?"

"Delusions almost always have some kind of internal logic," said Dr. Plath, "no matter how convoluted."

I looked up at her. "You think I'm delusional?"

Dr. Plath touched the end of her pen to her lips. "Was your time as a missionary when your behavior finally became criminal? We still haven't quite gotten there."

I leaned against the hard back of my industrial chair and sighed. "There's no real proselytizing allowed in Greece," I said. "We had to find sneaky ways to do it. That all contributed to my living a secret life. And we baptized so few people. I felt like a complete failure. I *hated* that my relatives were watching every single failure. I grew angrier and angrier, and that's when I started acting out."

"What did you do?"

"I had a companion who was gay, so I seduced him. I told Elder Carruthers, 'When in Greece...' and asked him to slide his penis inside me." I looked at Dr. Plath. "I'm not gay, you know. Well, maybe a little bi. But really, I just wanted to make my grandma upset so she'd leave me alone. Being entered reminded me of those times in the bathroom trying to push my stool back in. It was oddly comforting. After Elder Carruthers fucked me, I'd go to the bathroom and squeeze out his cum. I dared Grandma to watch. And she did."

"You *saw* her?" Dr. Plath tried to brush some hair behind her ear again but couldn't because obviously her hair still wasn't long enough. She may have felt this interview had gone on far too long, but we'd really only passed a few minutes together. How competent could she be as a psychiatrist, I wondered, if she couldn't even keep track of the length of her hair?

Who was going to help me if she didn't? I needed help.

Help!

Oh, God, hear the words of my mouth!

I shook my head. "My mom emailed me the very next day telling me she felt her parents' presence when she went to the temple and meditated in the Celestial Room. They assured her they were still watching me."

"Certainly," Dr. Plath said, "you realize—" She cut herself off.

"The problem," I went on, "is that I started getting off on *knowing* other people were watching. What had been such an inhibiting factor before became a stimulant. When Elder Carruthers was fucking me, I called out for my cousins to watch. I called for my great-aunts and great-uncles, for my great-grandparents."

I smiled as I remembered the thrill of realizing I had a full audience any time I did something naughty. Weak things had finally become strong unto me. "I started inviting Sophocles to watch. And Aristotle. And Helen of Troy."

Dr. Plath stopped writing and looked at me carefully again. Did *she* want to watch, I wondered?

It was exhausting being on stage every moment of one's life.

Perhaps the weak things were still weak.

"Of course, my companion freaked out and told the mission president everything, and I was sent home in shame." I remembered hiding my erection from my family with my Book of Mormon when I met them at the airport. "My mother's first words were, 'Your grandparents are very disappointed in you.' *She* wasn't disappointed, mind you, her dead parents were."

I clenched my fists for a moment and then relaxed them again, afraid of what Dr. Plath might think. "My stake president held a court, and I was excommunicated." I remembered my father sitting on the high council and feeling both his shame and mine at the same time. "Did you know, when you get ex'ed, they ask you to take off your garments?"

"Garments?"

"Mormon underwear. They expect you to step into another room to do it, but I stripped right in front of everyone." I chuckled. "They couldn't run out of there fast enough."

"That was funny to you?"

I shook my head. "It was...exciting."

Dr. Plath nodded.

"I started college soon after that. Had to move out, of course. My parents wouldn't let me live with them anymore." I shrugged. "At first, I masturbated in the campus bathrooms, moaning just loudly enough so that the other guys in the bathroom would know what I was doing. I was no longer satisfied only having invisible spirits watching. The problem with spirits is you can never really be sure they're there."

Dr. Plath wrote that down as well.

"I'm not crazy, you know. I realize perfectly well there may be no such thing as spirits." How many times, in fact, had I prayed for that to be true? How many hours on my knees?

I quickly discovered I could fuck the space between the top mattress and the bottom mattress while praying. Was Grandpa jealous that he couldn't get off anymore? Did Grandma miss the times her husband still poked her with a physical penis? If my body was a temple, perhaps I was doing proxy sex work for them.

"I needed real people now."

"So how long have you been exposing yourself in public, Noel?" Dr. Plath asked. She browsed through her notes. "You're finishing up your second year at college, I see." She'd obviously gathered some information on me before even starting the interview.

I nodded. "It began sometime during that freshman year." Soon moaning in the bathroom stall hadn't been enough. I stroked myself at the urinal next to someone pissing. I stroked myself in the park when old ladies like my grandma were feeding the pigeons. "You don't really need the details, do you? You've got what you came for. The origin of my illness."

"Noel," Dr. Plath said carefully, "I appreciate you being so candid. You've given me more than enough details. It's been very helpful. I'm curious about one thing, though."

"Yes?"

"If you're an exhibitionist, why didn't you just start acting in adult videos? You're certainly attractive enough."

I smiled. Dr. Plath *was* interested! I didn't know if that was a good thing or a bad one. I felt my groin twitch a little. "Pornography is a sin," I said.

She wrote something down. Then she looked up at me again. "You were arrested after one of your neighbors filmed you masturbating in the laundry room of your apartment building."

I nodded, ashamed and aroused. "It's not fair, you know. How can I help but be a sex offender when my own sweet grandmother is a slutty perv?" I'd begged Heavenly Father again and again to send the spirits away, to call them off, but only last week, Mom had phoned to announce her parents were still watching over me around the clock.

I'd hung up the phone.

Dr. Plath wrote silently for two or three minutes. I started rubbing my crotch underneath the table but stopped when she looked up.

"If I go to a mental hospital," I said, "I'll probably get a private room. If you just send me to prison, I know I'll beat off in front of my cellmate every day. I need to learn how to be private again."

Dr. Plath closed her notebook. "I'm going to need to consult with a colleague," she said, gathering her things. "Thank you again for speaking with me, Noel. The truth is we see disturbing behavior regularly in extremely devout members of many different religions. Sometimes, we can help. Sometimes..." She gave a half shrug. "I think we'll be able to help you."

Please let it be true, I prayed. Please, Heavenly Father. It was excruciating being this close to freedom. It was like seeing the bishop's wife at the grocery store and not being able to rub my crotch in the aisle. It was that moment right before ejaculation in the Faculty bathroom when my skin was chafing and I wasn't sure if the pain would keep me from cumming before a professor walked in.

And hoping the professor would walk in.

"Wait here, and I'll have a guard come retrieve you."

"They're watching me right now, you know."

Dr. Plath turned her head toward the mirror.

"No. *They*."

Dr. Plath looked at me a moment longer and then walked out of the room, closing the door firmly. I heard the lock click. I felt the air pressing in on me the way the water had when I groped myself in the Athens baptismal font while the woman I'd just baptized climbed out into my companion's helping arms. I felt the same choking sensation I experienced when forcing myself to eat a slice of the sacrament bread after ejaculating onto it.

"They're all watching!" I shouted after her.

But there was complete silence in the room once I stopped shouting. It was so peaceful being alone. I looked up in the corners of the room where the walls met the ceiling. But I knew I would never really be alone, not even if I was sent to solitary confinement. I jabbed my finger in the air. "Where are you, Grandma?" I shouted, breaking the silence.

I looked at the mirror on the wall and then back into the corners of the room. "You can't get enough, can you?" I shouted, stamping my foot.

"Stop watching me! Stop it!" I covered my eyes with both hands. "Stop it! Stop it! Stop it! Stop it!"

I dropped my pants and started masturbating.

Garbage Everywhere

"Eleanor, you should really look at these YouTube videos about the temple." Eleanor's friend Patty thrust the phone toward her.

"I don't want to see them," Eleanor said. "Why are you always showing me anti-Mormon stuff? I don't attack the Catholic Church, do I?"

"Yes, you do," Patty told her. The parrot in the cage nearest them squawked and flicked some bird seed onto the floor. Patty leaned down to brush it up.

Eleanor frowned. "When?" she demanded.

"You told me you read *The Da Vinci Code*."

"So?"

"So that means you're attacking the Catholic Church. That book is complete trash."

Eleanor sighed. It was possible her neighbor was right. Eleanor never did understand human interaction very well. At the sandwich shop where she worked part-time, a Black woman had called the boss to complain that Eleanor hadn't put her change directly into the woman's hand but had put it on the counter instead.

Both the customer's hands had been full at the time and Eleanor didn't want to make her feel she was being hurried, so she'd put the money down to be picked up when the woman was ready. Somehow, that had offended her. And it was possible, Eleanor thought, the customer had a right to feel offended. She just didn't know.

The voices used to warn her when she was doing something wrong. Of course, the voices pretty much told her everything she did was wrong. They told her she was too stupid to pass a math class. They told her she wasn't sexy enough to attract a good man. They said the reason her parents had killed themselves when she turned eighteen was because they were so embarrassed by her.

"Okay, Patty, I'm sorry," Eleanor said. She looked over toward one of the parrots, which seemed to glare back at her. "I need to get to the store now. I'll stop by later with your broccoli."

With that, Eleanor left Patty's apartment, walked next door to her own, and grabbed her grocery cart. They didn't really live in apartments, of course. They were houses, but they were small and run-down, and NAMI had found the places for both of them. Patty had lived here much longer, though, and seemed to feel this gave her the right to order other neighbors about. Eleanor had been homeless for a few months before she was finally diagnosed, but now she received Disability payments, and that was fortunately just barely enough to get by.

She didn't want Patty to complain about her and have NAMI move her somewhere else that might be even worse. Someone in the area kept throwing greasy pizza boxes in her yard on Friday nights, but in her previous apartment before she was kicked out, someone had often dumped used hypodermics.

The grocery was almost two miles away, and the sun was blazing. The view along the way wasn't particularly scenic, as Eleanor had to maneuver around an assortment of beer cans, fast food wrappers, used disposable diapers, and other trash in her path. There were a couple of styrofoam containers from some nearby restaurant, half a smashed chocolate bar, a dirty blanket, and a lone shoe. She tried to avoid the broken glass in the Safeway parking lot and the oil slicks from leaky motors.

Even inside the store, someone had eaten some fresh grapes and dropped the bare stem on the floor. Someone else had knocked a jar of spaghetti sauce off the shelf. A young man was mopping up the mess. Eleanor put two cases of Coke in her cart, some Ramen noodles, a bag of rice, some dry pinto beans, and Patty's frozen broccoli. Her EBT card paid for it all, but she was almost at her limit. She dropped the broccoli off at Patty's apartment and then went home.

Eleanor shopped for Patty a couple of times a week. Her neighbor was fifty years old, a good decade older than Eleanor, and weighed sixty-five pounds. The woman simply refused to eat. Or at least insisted on vomiting and using laxatives to combat the calories she did take in.

Eleanor had been forced to call an ambulance for Patty twice in the year she'd known her, but her neighbor kept hanging in there somehow. She'd made Eleanor promise to take care of her birds, all twelve of them, if she died. Eleanor had said yes, of course, so the woman wouldn't feel bad, but there was no way.

One of Patty's parrots always said, "Eleanor is a bitch," whenever Eleanor came over. The other parrots didn't insult her. At least to her face. Maybe she could take the well-mannered birds in.

Eleanor set the two cases of Coke on the living room floor and put the rest of the food in a cabinet. The floors in the living room and the kitchen were covered with empty Coke cartons and crumpled Coke cans. There were plastic grocery bags everywhere, even on top of the stove.

Catalogs she'd received in the mail lay scattered beside the TV and microwave and end table, along with dirty food wrappers from the sandwich shop. She got to make herself a sandwich to bring home the three evenings a week she worked there.

Eleanor supposed the real problem was all the dirty dishes on the counter and coffee table and floor. It was just too hard to wash them every day.

She was used to the roaches by now.

Eleanor grabbed a cold Coke from the refrigerator, took a long, refreshing sip, and then brushed some crumbs off the sofa so she could sit down. It was time to go over her Relief Society lesson. She only taught once a month, and this Sunday it was her turn. The lesson emphasized how important it was to encourage one's husband to lead the family in prayer.

Eleanor had more difficulty concentrating on the words than usual, unable to stop thinking of the news report yesterday describing how politicians were trashing services for the poor and sick. Successful people could sometimes be so mean.

They thought *she* was trash.

And maybe they were right. She wasn't pretty or smart. She hadn't even finished her second year of college. She still owed money for two payday loans she'd defaulted on before she'd been diagnosed. She'd been arrested once for stalking her boss at the last job she was fired from. But she didn't do things like that anymore, not since the voices no longer provoked her non-stop.

She might be damaged goods, she conceded, but she wasn't trash.

She bit her thumb. She just didn't understand the way normal people thought.

Eleanor read a few more paragraphs of the Relief Society lesson and closed her eyes, trying to grasp their meaning, planning how to sound profound in class. Maybe one day they'd make her a counselor. Perhaps even Relief Society president.

Sometime later, she awakened with a start when she heard a knock at the door. She kicked a Coke carton out of the way and stumbled to see who it was.

"Hi, Eleanor! How are you?"

It was the sister missionaries. "Oh, I'm fine," Eleanor said, her head still a bit foggy. It always felt a little foggy, though, even if she hadn't been napping. She was forever forgetting she had rice cooking, which was why her pots were so hard to clean. She kept forgetting to pay her electric bill and had to go down to the office almost every month to have it turned on again. "You working in this area today?"

"No." Sister Farnsworth smiled at her. "We came especially to see you." Sister Merrill smiled broadly as well.

Eleanor frowned. "Why?" She could never afford to invite them to dinner. She never had referrals to give them. She never went teaching with them when they asked.

The sisters laughed. "Because we love you!"

That seemed unlikely. Eleanor knew she was boring. She'd never gone through the temple, never gone on a mission, never married, never held an interesting job. She didn't want to talk about her miscarriage, or the time she was evicted for feeding stray cats, or how she'd slept with one of her landlords a couple of times when she didn't have the rent.

No one wanted to sleep with her now, of course. She'd grown fat over the years, only losing five pounds even when she was homeless. She never bothered with make-up anymore. She'd been inactive in the Church for ages, not coming back until she was on meds, and didn't know half of what the other women in Relief Society knew.

She didn't even seem to know half of what Patty knew about Mormons.

"That's sweet to say." Eleanor opened the door wider and ushered them in. As they walked into the house, though, she wondered if maybe they were letting her know they were lesbians. Was she missing more clues?

People were so confusing. But she didn't want to lead them on. Should she explain she was straight? That she was flattered but not interested? She'd said that to a couple of her female bosses over the years, and it never seemed to go well. It was only her male bosses, though, who wouldn't take no for an answer. Even after she started putting on weight.

"You're crazy," the last one had said as he put his hands under her blouse. "No one's going to believe you."

She still wasn't sure why she'd bit him after he thrust his penis into her mouth. She couldn't remember if it was one of the voices that had encouraged it or her own idea.

But being homeless was better than putting up with that any longer. And if she hadn't been homeless, she might not have attempted suicide, and if she hadn't attempted suicide, she might not have gotten that psychiatric evaluation.

"Have a seat," Eleanor said to the missionaries. "Do you want a Coke?"

The two sisters looked at each other. Eleanor had read that the Church finally okayed caffeinated soft drinks recently, but maybe the missionaries had stricter rules. "Oh, that's all right," said Sister Farnsworth, "we're not thirsty."

It was ninety-two degrees outside.

Eleanor brushed some crumbs off the part of the sofa that was still dirty and motioned toward the cushion.

"Eleanor," Sister Merrill said slowly, not moving to sit down, "do you mind if we help you clean up the place?"

"Oh, I can't ask you to do that."

"We don't mind."

Eleanor shrugged and spread her arms wide. "Be my guest." For the next two hours, the sisters picked up garbage, put away groceries, washed dishes, and mopped the floor. They even cleaned the bathroom, which was really a mess.

Eleanor felt guilty for not helping, but she focused on her Relief Society manual instead. She was such a lousy teacher. All she did was read from the book and ask the class questions. But if she didn't go over the lesson several times first, she'd get tongue-tied in front of everyone.

"Whew!" Sister Farnsworth put her hands on her hips. "That's better!"

"You want a Coke now?"

"No, we'd better get going."

"Oh, you have a teaching appointment?"

"Uh, no, but we still need to leave."

Eleanor nodded. "Okay." She smiled at them. She knew it was right to smile. "Thanks for stopping by!" The two young women hugged her and then walked off. She had to admit, the house looked great. The sisters who were stationed here before this pair had cleaned the place five or six months ago. Eleanor wasn't sure if she'd cleaned it herself any since then.

No, wait. She'd washed all the dirty dishes once about two months ago. You could eat on dirty dishes several times before it became too disgusting, but you had to clean them once in a while. She'd put the worst of the dirty pots outside, but after they sat out there for a few weeks, someone had taken them.

People were sure weird. It wasn't as if she'd put a "Free" sign on them or anything. Someone probably stole them to subsidize their drug habit. They'd left a splatter of vomit where the pots had been.

Eleanor went to the cabinet and pulled out a box of oatmeal cookies. Patty's sister collected expired cookies and other treats at work and gave some to Patty every few weeks, trying to fatten her up, and then Patty gave the ones she didn't like to Eleanor. Which was most of them.

Her food budget still never got her to the end of the month.

A roach crawled out of the box and scurried away. It wasn't entirely unattractive, she thought, the lovely color of cola. Patty kept telling her to buy some poison, but roaches needed love, too. Eleanor picked out the last three cookies, deliberately tossing a raisin on the floor, and put the empty box on the counter.

Then she sat on the sofa to eat while she watched *Ellen*. Ellen could always make her laugh, even when Eleanor didn't get the jokes. The woman just exuded humor and Eleanor couldn't help but giggle as she listened.

She'd loved reading novels for English class, too, but she'd never really understood those, either. Literature always required an understanding of people. She'd hoped the assignments would give her a stronger grasp on human psychology.

Her 1.2 average got her kicked out of the university.

But she always guessed the answers on *Wheel of Fortune* before the contestants did.

Most of the time, anyway.

She'd thrown all her Norton anthologies in the garbage years ago, too tired to pack and move them any longer. It seemed she had a new address every year.

She planned to stay in this place the rest of her life.

Eleanor heated some Ramen noodles and grabbed a Coke for dinner while she watched a few minutes of the news. Some white Christian had shot at a group of Sikhs, thinking they were Muslims. There was a clip of him shouting, "Arabs are the scum of the Earth!" Eleanor couldn't help but wonder what God thought of the shooter.

No one was trash to God.

Not even Eleanor.

She stared at her fat stomach and frowned.

Miri, one of her Visiting Teachers who gave her a ride to church most Sundays, said that if Eleanor had enough faith, she wouldn't need medication. Some of the other sisters in Relief Society said the same thing, but Eleanor would always just respond, "When I have enough faith, I'll stop taking the pills." No one ever knew quite what to say after that.

Eleanor watched a news segment about low-income residents in Detroit having their homes confiscated because of shady lending practices, their belongings thrown on the curb. She just didn't understand people.

During a commercial break, the phone rang. Eleanor sighed and pressed Talk. "Hi, Patty," she said. "What's up?"

"I forgot to ask for bird seed when you went to the store earlier."

"Oh, Patty, I asked you about that specifically."

"Do you mind going back?"

Eleanor closed her eyes. "Sure, it's not as hot now."

The trip there and back took almost ninety minutes, but it wasn't as if she didn't need the exercise. It was too bad she couldn't give some of her excess weight to Patty. When she knocked on the door, her neighbor waved Eleanor in and pointed to where she wanted her to set the bird seed.

"Eleanor is a bitch."

"I hate that bird, Patty."

"Oh, she's just joking."

Was that even possible, Eleanor wondered? She didn't much understand other species, either.

At least the mean voices she heard these days were real.

"Here," Patty said. "Have a box of cinnamon crunch donuts." She pulled a box out of her pantry. There were no roaches here.

"But those are your favorites," Eleanor protested. Not that Patty kept them down for long. The musty smell of birds in the apartment was always mingled with a hint of bile.

"My sister will get me some more. They just throw this stuff out where she works. And you've been so nice to me today."

So who taught the bird what to say?

"Thank you." Eleanor took the donuts.

"Wanna see what I found on the internet today about your church?"

Eleanor shook her head. "Not tonight."

"It's all about how Joseph Smith tricked people into saying they'd seen the gold plates."

"Those are all lies people made up."

"I just don't want to see you keep paying tithing to a false church."

"The Church gives me a delivery of food every month." Which still wasn't enough to get her to her next Disability check. "It helped me get this job at the sandwich shop."

Patty pursed her lips and nodded. "Okay, Eleanor. Okay."

Eleanor leaned over to give Patty a hug, feeling her bones through the clothing. Why didn't Catholic Charities help the woman get counseling so she'd start to eat again? Patty was always talking about the help they gave her, but whatever they did, it wasn't enough. Wouldn't a church led by God be able to really help the suffering?

"I need to take a shower so I'll be ready for work tomorrow. My days off seem to go so fast now that I'm back in the workforce."

"Don't earn too much," Patty warned.

"I won't."

Back in her own apartment, Eleanor went over her Relief Society lesson once again. It had felt so good three months ago when she was called to help teach, her first calling since going back to church. They liked her. They needed her.

Who even cared if the Church wasn't true? The voices had told her as much years and years ago. Even with her meds now, one lone voice still spoke to her sometimes, usually in Sacrament meeting, and it always told her the same thing.

But it didn't matter.

Eleanor had heard that the previous bishop of her ward had been excommunicated for having an affair with one of the Sunday School teachers. But that was no worse than Patty's priest being accused of molesting one of the altar boys. That Mormon White House secretary lost his job a few months ago for beating both his first and second wife.

But she'd seen a picture of the Pope hugging a girl with Down Syndrome. And Miri volunteered at the Bishop's Storehouse every other week.

It was funny, but even Eleanor volunteered to pick up trash in the park once a month. When she'd told Miri, Miri had just laughed.

After she reported to her psychiatrist overhearing two nuns at the sandwich shop plotting to steal all the frozen bread to feed the pigeons, the doctor increased her dosage. The next day on the news, she saw that a "family values" politican had been caught hiring a male escort. She wasn't even sure if she was still hallucinating or not.

It wasn't fair. She could have been such a great person. A scientist. A fashion designer. A poet.

A wife and mother.

The Church said she should still aim for the Celestial Kingdom. Maybe the voice she heard every week in the chapel was lying to her. But she knew even if the Church was true, she'd only be tossed from the presence of all the gods mingling in the highest level and end up with the other rejects in the Telestial Kingdom.

The garbage dump of heaven. That's what happened to people like her. She might not understand humans, but she understood God.

Eleanor leaned back against the sofa and hugged the Relief Society manual to her chest like a lover. She watched a roach crawl around the lid of the Coke she'd had earlier for dinner and realized her mouth felt dry. Maybe there was a little soft drink left. She leaned forward, gently brushed her companion away, and took a sip.

The Dissociative Singularity of the Gods

I cleared my throat. Then I cleared it again. And again. And again.

"What is wrong with you?" Mom asked, more with a look of irritation than concern. She put down her fork and passed my sister the salt. Susan ignored me, as usual. At fifteen, she was a year younger than I was, but when we did interact, she liked to repeat that girls matured emotionally much earlier than boys. I usually responded by asking if that was why she seemed increasingly senile.

"Nothing," I said, scooping up another spoonful of peas. Mom loved English peas and served them every single day of the week, even with Chinese or Mexican food. That was what first got me interested in OCD and other disorders.

"You've been doing that a lot lately," Dad said, clearing his throat in an exaggerated fashion. He usually let Mom do most of the day-to-day parenting, reserving as his contribution to our governance the power to punish any infraction of the rules.

When I was in first grade, he'd withdrawn me from the school Christmas play ten minutes before I was supposed to go on, "to teach me a lesson," even though that meant everyone else in the class suffered, too. I had no recollection, naturally, of the lesson I was supposed to have learned.

I shrugged. Then I shrugged a second time. And a third. And once again.

"Stop it!" Mom demanded, accidentally spitting a pea into her milk.

"Sorry," I said. "Sorry. Sorry. Sorry. Sorry. Sorry."

"Ryan," Dad said, his jaw clenched, "go to your room."

I shoved one last bite of food in my mouth and left the table. As I closed my bedroom door, though, I broke out in a smile. My plan seemed to be working. Soon I'd be free. Or at least freer. My smile faded, however, as I realized success tonight meant no food until the following morning. I'd have to start stashing snacks in my sock drawer in case I was banished from the dinner table again.

At least Mom and Dad were noticing, though. And with Dad's ability to detach, that was saying something. I'd been slowly developing tics over the last several weeks after doing some research online. It was excruciating to work this slowly, but I had to be meticulous in laying the groundwork if I wanted to succeed.

I wasn't allowed to stream anything on my phone, and I didn't feel like reading, though I was part way through three different books. Might as well work on my paper for History. I'd seen the movie *Frances* at my friend Martin's house a couple of weeks ago and decided to write about the unethical treatment of the mentally ill, especially those labeled mentally ill who really weren't.

Of course, people with Tourette's weren't typically successful at schoolwork, so writing a good paper only made my case less convincing, but I couldn't help it. I liked doing well at my studies. I hadn't seen the movie *One Flew Over the Cuckoo's Nest* yet, but I'd checked the book out of the school library. It was one of those I was halfway through. Martin promised we'd watch Milos Forman's film soon, but he didn't like watching too many heavy movies in a row.

We watched *Arsenic and Old Lace*, for instance, the week after we'd seen *The Snake Pit*. We watched *Miss Congeniality* the week after *Silver Linings Playbook*, *Sister Act* the week after *Ordinary People*.

After working on my paper for an hour, I heard a timid knock on the bedroom door, and Mom stuck her head in. "I thought you might want this," she said softly, looking over her shoulder before entering the room. She set a plate on my desk with the remains of my dinner.

"It's cold," she said, "but I can't defy your father completely." Dad had never hit Mom, but he did tell us every so often about how his grandfather killed his grandmother and then himself when they were both in their seventies. Dad never really made any point when he repeated the story, just letting the information hang there.

"Thanks, Mom."

She smiled and glided out of the room quietly.

I slept better on a full stomach, but the alarm still sounded like a wailing Banshee the next morning. I thought about the scene from *Private Benjamin* which I'd watched with Martin several months ago, the week after we'd watched *American Psycho*, where the Goldie Hawn character tells her drill sergeant, "There are no curtains on these windows! I'll be up at the crack of dawn!"

I wondered if the Church forced not only its teenagers attending Seminary but also missionaries serving their missions to wake up so ridiculously early for the same reason the military insisted recruits do. I'd once overheard my uncle telling my dad he refused to be "Church-broke." Dad didn't talk to his brother for the last two years before my uncle committed suicide.

Their father had killed himself as well, shortly before I was born.

Thank goodness I'd never felt depressed, though religion certainly added unnecessary stress to my life. I decided over a year ago that even if there were a God, he had nothing to do with us any longer. Just as humans had created computers and both anticipated and feared the day of the singularity when an artificial intelligence gained self-awareness along with the capacity to enhance and promote its own destiny, God had created life on Earth, and it had culminated in humans reaching their own singularity several thousand years ago. We were now in control of our own lives.

The biggest glitch in our software seemed to be the need for almost every individual human to try controlling every other human, no matter what the cost.

I thought it clear that the reason Mormon teenagers were ordered to wake up so early was a result of the leaders in Salt Lake trying to keep us too busy to think of anything besides church. But even in Seminary, I studied my Biology notes. I planned to do my science project this year on the effects of labeling on teenage girls.

Of course, I only had the one subject, and no control, but I wasn't publishing my results, just trying to do something not entirely boring. My sister didn't need to know that every time she hesitated when searching for a word, and I interrupted to ask if she was developing dementia, that I was timing to see if her hesitations grew longer or shorter or stayed the same as the labeling progressed.

One Mississippi, two Mississippi, three Mississippi...

Susan and I slowly chomped on our cereal this morning like zombies. Susan usually ate Honey Nut Cheerios. I preferred Frosted Mini-Wheats. I couldn't figure out a way to annoy her about that today and so simply made sure to sniff loudly after every bite.

Mom could apparently hear me over the sizzling bacon she was carefully preparing for Dad's breakfast. He would only kiss her goodbye in the morning if he was satisfied that day with his bacon, which he seemed to love as much as Mom loved peas. "You getting a cold, Ryan?"

"No, I'm fine." I sniffed again. And again. Susan gave me the evil eye.

A few minutes later, we grabbed our books and climbed into Sister Baldwin's car. Nancy Baldwin was Susan's best friend at church. They did all their Personal Progress steps for Young Women at the same time. Sister Baldwin drove the three of us to the ward meetinghouse for Seminary, where we then dragged ourselves up the walkway.

Sleep deprivation could cause psychotic episodes, I remembered. That probably explained Jack, the son of the Relief Society president, whose eyes darted around like fireflies whenever I looked at him during class.

Maybe he was plotting his own escape.

Sister Sorenson started the lesson right on time, smiling as if she'd been awake for hours already. I couldn't help but wonder if she was obeying the Word of Wisdom. It was too soon to move to the final stage of my plans, but I didn't think I could take early morning Seminary much longer. Especially now that Cindy was no longer attending.

She was a lovely girl from my Sunday School class. Susan had never liked Cindy, of course, and enjoyed reminding me that the object of my desire was rumored to have paid the Laurel instructor a hundred dollars to check off two different categories on her Personal Progress report which she didn't feel like completing in real life.

I rather liked seeing her take control of her own destiny. I wondered if there was a second level of actualization humans might reach someday. A second singularity. Perhaps that was the motivation behind science fiction stories set in the distant future. Wouldn't it be incredible, I thought, to spend a lifetime studying the possibility?

Was that what Mormons meant when they talked about becoming gods?

In every myth, there was usually a kernel of truth. Maybe the early Church leaders had tentatively grasped this evolutionary concept, even before Darwin published his infamous book.

Andrew started the opening prayer. Sister Sorenson called on him more than anyone else. He was the bishop's son. "Dear Heavenly Father," he began, "we thank thee for this wonderful weather. We thank thee for this blessed opportunity to study thy gospel, and we thank thee for the dedication of Sister Sorenson who prepared the lesson for our benefit. We ask thee—"

"Shit!"

Andrew stopped speaking. I opened my eyes to see everyone in class staring at me. Even Susan looked concerned. More suspicious, of course, than worried. "Sorry," I said. "Sorry. Sorry. Sorry. Sorry. Sorry."

"Are you feeling okay?" Sister Sorenson asked, her eyebrows furrowed.

"Shit!" I shouted again.

"Ryan, you'd better wait out in the foyer until your ride to school comes."

I made every effort not to smile as I gathered my things.

"Susan will go over with you later what we cover in class so you can still take the test on Monday."

It took no effort not to smile now.

An hour later, Susan joined me in the foyer. "What are you playing at?" she whispered.

"What do you mean?"

"You know damn well what I mean."

"Susan," I said, "your language."

Her eyes narrowed, and for a moment I thought she was going to hit me with her backpack. I'd seen her kick the neighbor's poodle once when it crapped in our yard and could still hear its pitiful yelp in my mind every night. But instead she motioned with a sharp jerk of the chin, and Nancy and I followed her outside to Mom's car. Mom always took the second shift, driving us to school after Seminary was over for the day. Neither Susan nor Nancy said anything about what had happened in class.

School went well enough, the best part of every day. It would undoubtedly be even more satisfying once Seminary was a thing of the past. I enjoyed all my classes, including Physics, though our teacher could rival Ben Stein's presentation in *Ferris Bueller* any day.

In P.E., I had a chance to talk to Martin, still the only non-LDS friend my parents would permit me to socialize with. That would stop, I knew, if they discovered our R-rated sins. We'd watched *Split* last weekend.

"Tomorrow's Saturday," I said. "Are we still on for a movie?"

"How does *The Visit* sound?"

"M. Night Shyamalan?"

Martin laughed. "You know a lot for a culturally deprived Mormon."

"Don't tell my sister." I laughed as well, happy for two psychological movies in a row. I wasn't about to question Martin's change of heart.

But my movie plans didn't work out. Susan reported my cursing episode from Seminary while the family gathered together for spaghetti that evening. Spaghetti with a side of English peas, naturally. Mom looked horrified at the news, though Dad just seemed angry. He stabbed his fork into the table an inch from my hand.

"I don't know what's gotten into you lately, young man, but you're grounded for the next two weeks. You'll go to Seminary, you'll go to school, and you'll go to church, but nothing else. And if you act up again, I'll take away your phone."

I was tempted to curse right then, but I held my tongue. I'd known this would be the next step in my plan, but that didn't make it any easier. "Sure, Dad," I said, letting my head hang. "I don't know what's wrong with me, either."

"Maybe..." Mom said, her voice shaking, "maybe he's possessed? Do you think he needs a priesthood blessing?"

"He's not possessed," Susan stated flatly.

"Maybe all he needs is to see a doctor?" Mom sounded more hopeful now.

"What he needs is a good spanking," said Dad. "Something that will leave marks. Kids today are so spoiled."

"Hey!" Susan protested. "What did I do?"

"I want you both to go to your rooms after dinner and read your scriptures until bedtime." Dad calmly stuffed a meatball in his mouth and deliberately chewed with his mouth open. Susan glared at me across the table. I thought she was going to flick a pea at me. I frowned as she clenched her fork. Thank goodness we weren't having steak tonight.

"Sorry," I said. "Sorry. Sorry. Sorry. Sorry. Sorry."

Dad slapped the table so hard my milk glass tipped over. He swallowed his meatball and pointed in the direction of the hallway. "Ryan, you can get started right now."

As I stood up to leave, I could see by the look on Mom's face that she wouldn't be sneaking any food into my room later. Fortunately, I'd bought some peanut butter crackers after school today for just such an eventuality.

Of course, I didn't spend the rest of the evening reading the Book of Mormon as ordered. I kept it open on my desk in case Mom or Dad popped in unannounced, but I spent most of my time working on my History paper again. If I kept up my grades until I graduated next year, I might be able to win a scholarship. I knew Dad would only pay for school if I went to Brigham Young. And he would only pay for Brigham Young if I served a mission first.

I couldn't wait to move to the other side of the country and make a life for myself.

At 9:25, just before my mandated bedtime, I went down to the kitchen. I liked to be a little noisy at times like this so that Susan, who had to be in bed by 9:00, could hear I was still up.

"No food!" Dad shouted from the living room.

"Just getting a glass of water."

"No food and no drink!" Dad shouted. "You need to learn your lesson!"

"You don't want my kidneys to fail, do you?"

I heard Mom murmuring something to him and Dad grunting in reply. But neither of them said anything more, so I drank while I had the chance. I supposed I might better start sneaking bottled water into my bedroom, too.

Martin was disappointed I couldn't come over the following morning as we'd planned, but I doubted he missed me as much as I missed him. He was free all the time while our few hours together were the only freedom I ever enjoyed away from school. We always played a game of chess each Saturday while we listened to Beyoncé before settling down to our movie of the week.

"I could sneak you my old iPad," he said. "That way you can stream whatever you want without worrying." He knew my dad checked my personal devices regularly.

"It's more fun to watch with you," I said. It was like drinking hot chocolate at Starbucks versus drinking it at home. "This too shall pass."

I spent most of my Martinless Saturday morning studying for school, which wasn't a bad alternative, and then, after lunch, I went ahead and studied for Seminary, too. I just didn't like getting any bad grades, even in classes I didn't want to take.

Finally, to reward myself, I finished reading Ken Kesey's book and then went to the bathroom and beat off while thinking of ex-Seminary student Cindy. At least I'd see her at church tomorrow. Though if my plan was successful, I wouldn't even be seeing her there much longer.

There was no way to go to the store while being grounded, but I did sneak some Pop Tarts and a pudding cup from the kitchen into my room, knowing I'd need them the next day. I smuggled in a can of Sprite later as well. It was too bad healthy foods were harder to conceal. I certainly couldn't hide a chicken breast in my closet. Or a tub of cottage cheese.

Susan passed by the kitchen to grab a glass of milk during my last foray and caught me slipping a tiny can of fatty Vienna sausage into my pants. "What are you doing with that…?"

"That…?" I looked at her quizzically. "How's the dementia coming along, Sis?"

One Mississippi, two Mississippi.

"One of these days…"

I grinned. "Dementia making it hard to finish that sentence?"

I was a model of silent obedience during dinner that night. My parents looked pleased but wary. Susan ignored me. Which was rather decent of her, since she could have turned me in. Perhaps, I thought, I should draw my science project to a close and give her a break.

Soon, I told myself. Soon. I wanted the findings from my flawed experiment to at least be entertaining enough to garner me an A for originality.

I thought about Cornelia Wilbur and Flora Rheta Schreiber faking most of their findings about Sybil.

And that made me wonder if real dissociative disorders were the next singularity. Becoming more than one sentient being. The Church never talked about that. The only multiple sentient beings working together as a unit that the Church ever mentioned were plural wives. Not the same thing at all.

But maybe based on the same kernel of truth?

It would relieve the stress a lot of Mormons felt if Celestial marriage were really only monogamy, just with each partner hosting a score or two of various personalities.

Sunday morning dawned bright and clear. I pulled my tie extra tight as we prepared for church, remembering that snug collars were a trigger for people with Tourette's. My biggest problem pulling off this medical charade was that most kids began showing symptoms much earlier than I was. Even late bloomers were demonstrating tics by their early teens.

But there were a small percentage of patients who started as late as I was pretending to. The good thing about my "case" was that the disease was harder to definitively diagnose when the onset was so atypical. That would be in my favor when my folks were inevitably forced to seek a professional opinion. Even with routine symptoms, one couldn't assume Tourette's until the patient had been exhibiting for at least a year. There weren't even any lab tests which would help pin it down.

I thought about how Randle McMurphy's plan ended.

The stakes didn't seem quite as high for me, though the possibility of avoiding another year of Seminary, two years as a full-time missionary, and an additional four years at BYU seemed worth taking almost any risk. Fortunately, Tourette's was far more common in boys than girls. The best part was that the majority of cases seemed to resolve by the time those afflicted were in their late teens or early twenties. If I could just keep faking until after I'd missed my mission, I could then go back to behaving normally.

Assuming that after five or six years of faking, I'd be able to retrain myself. At least I wasn't trying to pretend at school. That gave me several hours of relative normalcy every day even now. If my parents asked why I was able to control my impulses there, I had my answer ready.

"Tics are more acute when a patient is especially stressed or anxious. I love school. I'm not stressed there." Of course, that would naturally lead to a discussion of why I felt stressed by Seminary and church and the thought of a mission.

I didn't have a good answer for that yet, since I doubted they wanted to hear the truth. Denial was a component of so many different conditions.

"Everybody in the car," Dad said, grabbing his scriptures. He insisted that people who chose to only bring phones with scripture apps would, come Judgment Day, achieve no higher than ministering angel status. They were clearly trying to sneak in some sports, if they were male, or shopping, if they were female.

I was sure the close-mindedness encouraged by most religions was a primary reason humans hadn't evolved to our next state. As I walked past my father with my own set of scriptures, he grabbed my shoulder and hissed, "You better behave, young man, or there will be hell to pay."

"Hell," I said. "Hell. Hell. Hell. Hell. Hell."

Dad's face turned almost purple, his eyes glazing over, but he didn't say anything.

I was legitimately frightened, though, and flinched. I wondered what Nephi thought the first time he realized Laman wasn't just angry but mad enough to kill him. Then I remembered that neither Nephi nor Laman was real. "I'll be good," I said. "I promise." I tried pretending it was a separate personality doing the lying but I was fully aware it was me.

Were people who believed that soap opera characters were real any crazier than the average Mormon, I wondered, who also believed in fictional characters? Was that true of the average Christian as well? Or Muslim? Or Jew? Or Hindu?

But if the majority of people on the planet were delusional, what constituted normality? Perhaps it was the person who *didn't* believe who exhibited abnormal psychology. I wished I knew which of those two populations was more likely to evolve.

In Sacrament meeting, our family liked to sit about four rows back from the podium, right in the middle of the pew. I sat on the left side of my dad today, as usual, my mom to his right, and Susan to her right. I behaved reverently through the opening hymn and opening prayer. I even sat quietly during the sacrament hymn and then as the bread was blessed and passed. As one of five active priests in the ward, I took part in blessing the sacrament in front of the congregation every other week.

I'd hoped to show my most blatant disqualifying symptoms on a Sunday when I was reading the prayer card myself. That would have been far more dramatic. But it couldn't be helped. After all this build up, I had to do something today.

As Andrew finished the prayer over the water, I said "Amen!" as loudly as I could. "Amen! Amen! Amen! Amen! Amen!"

Both priests, the bishop on the stand, the chorister, and the organist all looked in my direction. Dad dug his fingers into my arm so hard I almost shouted. After a moment of indecision, the priests nodded for the deacons to approach, and the second round of sacrament trays made its way about the chapel.

Cindy was the youth speaker after the priests and teachers joined their families down in the pews. I admired the way she had talked her parents out of making her attend Seminary and hoped to learn something helpful from her prepared message today. She was well-spoken if nothing else. And also reliably useful as a tool to aggravate Susan. I often pointed out Cindy's thick blond hair, her impeccable fashion sense, her success appearing in a TV commercial for her dad's car dealership, and the red Taurus her father had bought her.

I always wrote down Susan's reaction to my taunts, sure I could use them at some later date in a paper.

I wondered again if there might be something wrong with me psychologically, even if it wasn't Tourette's.

Cindy's talk was on humility. I doubted that was irony on her part. It was more likely an attempt by the bishop to keep her from becoming too worldly.

The natural man was an enemy to God.

Was it because we were no longer microorganisms?

It didn't feel wrong to want a career that let me contribute something meaningful to the advancement of mankind. To be someone like Freud or Erickson or Jung or Frankl or Laing or Kubler-Ross. To reveal a deeper understanding of the mind that allowed us to direct our own mental evolution.

I looked at my watch and groaned silently. Another half hour before the meeting ended, and there would be another two long hours of classes after that. How much precious time had I already wasted at church over the years? And it still hadn't been effective even at teaching me basic honesty. Or kindness. I wondered if I was without conscience. And then wondered how that might affect my career in psychiatry.

Might it be an asset?

I was going to have a nervous breakdown if I didn't do something soon.

I made a mental note to talk to a school counselor about seeing a psychiatrist. There was no reason I couldn't use that experience to write a better college application essay when the time came. Instead of the old, "Doctors Make the Worst Patients," I could proclaim "Patients Make the Best Doctors."

Was that why Church leaders always said the Church was a hospital for the sick?

The sick leading the sick?

If I was leaving the Church, I needed to make a clean break. I couldn't allow nostalgia to keep me connected to this mindset. *Homo sapiens* had continued to mate with Neanderthals for a while, but at some point, *Homo erectus* had to be left behind.

I thought of Tim LaHaye's novel *Left Behind*, which had been made into a movie Martin and I had watched once for laughs. So many different traditions insisted that at least some of us were moving to a higher plane. Didn't Jehovah's Witnesses think it would be a select 144,000?

I was going to meet an intelligent woman in graduate school, maybe one of my professors. She'd appreciate my intellect and I'd appreciate hers. We'd combine the best of our genes in our offspring. I couldn't let my life be ruled by superstition any longer.

Though it was odd that humans, the highest order of life on the planet, were the only species that *did* believe in superstition. What in the world did *that* suggest?

"And this," said Cindy, "is why humility is the most basic foundation for—"

"Fuck humility!"

Cindy stood at the podium, stunned, while the entire chapel erupted in a loud, uniform gasp. Dad gripped my arm so tightly I was sure he'd broken some blood vessels. He pulled me to my feet and dragged me out of the chapel, my scriptures falling to the floor. Everyone's eyes followed my exit.

This must have been what Nephi felt when Laman and Lemuel tied him up on the boat.

No. What Frances Farmer felt when she was carted off to an asylum. I thought about the many women in medieval Europe who'd been accused of witchcraft and killed because they refused to accept the role religion and society had chosen for them.

Dad and I didn't stop in the foyer. He dragged me into the boy's bathroom and pushed me up against a stall door. "I've had all I'm going to take from you, young man. You are going to regret—"

"I think I have Tourette's, Dad," I said. "You need to take me to a doctor."

Dad's mouth hung open as he tried to process what I'd just said.

"Tourette's is a disorder that—"

"So you're mentally deficient," he said in a cool, matter-of-fact tone. "Your mom was right." He shook his head. "But you didn't get this from me." He looked down at his crotch for a moment. "There's no madness in my family." He stared dully at the metal door behind me. "No madness."

"It's not the end of the world, Dad. In a few years—"

My father's grip on my arm grew even tighter, and I grimaced. He shoved the stall door open, turned me around, and forced me to my knees. "Dad!" The pain was excruciating. I wondered if he'd fractured one of my kneecaps.

Why hadn't I thought to file for legal emancipation in court? Maybe Martin's parents would let me live with them.

Odd how one's mind seemed to work so much better during a crisis. Like the way Abinadi testified so boldly to King Noah.

Stop it!

"I can't allow you to deny the Holy Ghost," Dad said calmly. "It's the most grievous sin." His fingers dug into my shoulders. "My father killed his parents when they wanted to leave the Church. My brother Jack killed our father when our father wanted to leave. I killed your uncle when he wouldn't come back."

This isn't normal, I kept telling myself. People aren't like this. He was putting on a charade, too.

I thought of all the men who killed women trying to leave them. I thought about East Germans back in the day killing those trying to escape Berlin, North Koreans killing those trying to defect to the south today.

My brain was working on a heightened level, my thoughts flashing by in nanoseconds. It was thrilling.

But now I remembered hearing rumors about Porter Rockwell, a Danite whose job in the early church was to kill apostates. And my History teacher had mentioned the book *Blood Atonement* one day in class. The events in that book had taken place only a few years ago.

It had never occurred to me before that an entire organization as an entity might be mentally unstable. With multiple personalities, one sociopathic, one paranoid. One loving, one manipulative, one cruel.

With how many other personalities?

Maybe it was mental illness which put people on a higher plane. Perhaps some type of mass hysteria which helped the entire species make great leaps forward. What a great topic for a paper, I thought. I felt on the verge of—

"The apostasy stops now."

I listened to the timbre of his voice in a detached manner, as if he were a patient in my office who'd come in for counseling, unable to see the bigger picture. He was living in the past.

It was the future that was important.

"I should have killed you before you turned eight."

The detachment dissipated as I realized that what was happening wasn't theoretical, as the thoughts I'd believed were so fast finally caught up with reality. I felt a flush of adrenaline that made my heart hurt and my mind go blank. "Shit!" I shouted. The profane language of the unenlightened.

My father stood behind me and pushed on my shoulders and head with all his weight, until my whole world was the toilet bowl. I could see the stains the ward volunteers had failed to clean away the day before. I resisted as best I could but after only a moment was unable to keep my face above the water any longer.

My head fully immersed, I kept trying to push myself up but simply couldn't get any leverage. I tried to shout and instead lost more air.

I could vaguely hear a noise I assumed was Dad speaking, but I couldn't make out the words.

My father's strength seemed to increase as mine diminished. He was pushing down so hard. I saw Cindy's face, which wasn't as pretty as I remembered. Then I thought of Martin. And Mom. Who really had always meant well.

Wasn't the bishop supposed to have the power of discernment? He should have ordered my father locked up ages ago.

How could he, though, if the priesthood wasn't real? What kind of pathetic charade was my Tourette's, when Mormon men pretended en masse to be prophets and apostles and judges in Israel? My fear turned to anger, but even that didn't give my muscles the extra strength they needed.

I held my breath as long as I could, a steady, calm part of my brain wondering if I was finally about to reach the next level of my existence.

But just at the end, as my vision grew dark, I had no choice but to accept the singular, inevitable fact about life, feeling a brief moment of peace when I realized that facing the ultimate truth put me at the highest elevation a human mind was capable of attaining.

And it still meant nothing.

Foreseeing the Future

"So, Craig," Bishop Harrington said in a somber tone, "do you masturbate?"

Ugh. I hated that question. We'd made it almost to the end of our interview without the unpleasant subject being raised. I thought maybe the new bishop wouldn't be too bad. He'd been ordained four months earlier, but this was my first private meeting with him.

"No, sir," I said. I'd been ordained a priest by my father under the direction of the previous leader of our ward, Bishop Whitford. He'd been a totally cool guy, but even he always asked about masturbation. These days when we met in the hallway at church, he just clapped me on the shoulder and said, "Hope everything is going okay."

But he never actually *asked* me how I was. Bishops were always called Bishop, I remembered, even after they were released from their calling. My dad was still gunning for the position himself, though Bishop Harrington would probably serve for at least the next three or four years.

"In fact, Bishop," I added, "I've *never* masturbated."

Bishop Harrington frowned. "Never, Craig?" he asked. "I find that hard to believe."

"Have you ever drunk a beer?" I asked in return.

"Certainly not."

"Well, I've never masturbated." He still looked unconvinced, so I added, "You do have the power of discernment, right?"

"Of course I do." He looked a bit offended I'd even asked such a question.

"My father warned me about masturbation before I was old enough to start," I explained, "so I never started."

"You're never too young," the bishop said. "Age only affects whether you ejaculate or not." For the head of a small PR firm, he seemed to know an awful lot about biology. Our leaders warned the youth constantly about the importance of avoiding pornography, and yet I sometimes wondered if these interviews weren't a bit pornographic themselves.

"Nevertheless." It was one of my favorite lines from *The African Queen.*

Bishop Harrington closed his eyes and sighed. "Craig," he said, now looking directly into my own eyes, "*every* boy masturbates. You just have to confess if you want to be forgiven."

Now it was my turn to frown. "Every boy?" I repeated. "You mean, Joseph Smith masturbated? And Brigham Young? And all the other prophets and apostles? David O. McKay? Gordon B. Hinckley?" I paused. "Boyd K. Packer?" I watched as the bishop's eyes narrowed. "*You* used to masturbate?" His earlier comment made sense now.

Bishop Harrington sat back in his chair, his hands clasped in front of him. "I can see you're going to be a hard case, Craig. But I promise you, I'm harder."

The interview was soon over, and I joined my parents and sister in the meetinghouse foyer. Services had let out, and they'd been waiting patiently while I saw the bishop. I'd been his third interview this afternoon. The wait gave Dad a chance to try out any new jokes he might have heard in the High Priests group on Mom and Arlene.

The one he learned last week had the punch line, "And then the Relief Society president spit on the casserole!" Mom had smiled politely. Arlene had offered what sounded like a genuine laugh, and I did my best to fake it.

Mom jumped to her feet when she saw me approaching down the hallway.

"Can we go home and eat now?" asked my sister, tapping her foot.

So much for patience.

Arlene was three years younger than I was and had only been interviewed twice, both times by Bishop Whitford. I was an old pro these days, having endured nine turns on the witness stand. I was surprised how difficult my sessions were, given that I never had any major sins to confess, was a model student at school, and a model Aaronic priesthood holder at church.

It was true enough I'd never masturbated. It wasn't just a lie to get the bishop off my back. I felt masturbating would kickstart my sexuality, and there was no point doing that. It was why I hadn't begun dating yet, either. I still had to finish high school and a mission before I could allow myself to be distracted.

Frankly, despite the Church's instruction to marry young, I didn't plan to start dating till after college. I wanted good grades. There was all of eternity to have sex. I needed a clear mind to earn a solid education and land a good job. Positions in my field weren't easy to come by.

A couple of weeks passed with nothing further of note to report. I was reading *Great Expectations* for school and was appalled that Dickens apparently thought having Pip marry Estella provided a happy ending for his readers.

Definitely proof that postponing dating was a good idea. In Chemistry, we made aspirin, leading my mother to bemoan the fact that "School will soon be teaching you to cook meth!" And in History, we learned about Wounded Knee.

Even the fact that Lamanites had fallen away from the gospel didn't quite seem to justify what happened there. At least Native Americans still had a glorious future ahead of them.

"You ready to see the stake patriarch?" my dad asked me after dinner one evening. "Your appointment's at 7:00."

"Sure," I said. "Let me brush my teeth first." We'd had spinach with dinner. Mom included fresh vegetables with every meal. I was completely on board with that, but Arlene often complained afterward that *she* was never going to inflict such things on *her* children.

I wouldn't, either, for different reasons.

"Get a move on. You don't want an angry patriarch foretelling your destiny."

Actually, I didn't want a Patriarchal Blessing at all. Most of my friends at church had already received theirs, but they were forbidden to share the details with anyone. All Devin would say was, "I've just *got* to be good if I want..." and never finish the sentence.

Heather would say, "At least I know how many babies I need to have." She'd never reveal the foreordained number, of course. Patriarchal Blessings were sacred, like the temple. Something you couldn't talk about casually.

Dad drove me a couple of miles to Brother Mason's house. His wife entertained Dad in the living room while Brother Mason and I went to his study. Men and women weren't supposed to be alone together without chaperones, but Brother Mason didn't seem concerned.

I could hear my dad start to tell Sister Mason one of his lame jokes as I followed her husband down the hall, sending up a quick prayer that this meeting wouldn't take too long.

"Tell me a little about yourself, young man," Brother Mason said genially, motioning to me with his right palm facing up.

"Well, for starters, my name is Craig," I began. It wasn't clear he remembered, and if I had to get a blessing, I wanted to make sure it was for the right person. I really thought life might be more of an adventure if I didn't know what to expect. Perhaps I shouldn't have clarified my name. It might have been better to get a blessing intended for someone else and still leave my own future uncharted.

"I like music," I continued. "I play the French horn at school and I'm teaching myself the trumpet and piccolo on my own. I'd love to play in a symphony one day."

Brother Mason wrinkled his nose. "Can you support a family on that?"

"If I get hired."

"What are some of your spiritual goals, young man?"

Sounded like I was back to being a generic youth. Better not to fight it. But the truth was I did have one specific goal in regard to church. "I'd like to go to the Czech Republic on my mission."

Brother Mason's eyebrows rose to the top of his forehead. "Whatever for?"

"I've just always felt that was where the Lord wanted me. I even bought a beginner's grammar book to help me establish a firm foundation before I go to the Missionary Training Center."

I couldn't very well tell him I wanted to go to Prague simply because I loved Dvořák. Leaders in Salt Lake might go out of their way to deliberately *not* send me if they suspected I wanted to go for secular reasons. If I could get Brother Mason to say something about the Czech Republic in my blessing, though, that might help me out two years from now when I had to submit my papers.

The interview continued another fifteen minutes. I understood that being informed made inspiration easier to recognize, but I couldn't help but think of Whoopi Goldberg from *Ghost*.

"You are from the tribe of Manasseh," Brother Mason said a moment after laying his hands on my head. He was recording the blessing so his wife could transcribe it for me later.

I knew most Mormons ended up in the tribe of Ephraim, even Charles, another priest in my quorum whose Jewish parents had converted when he was three. Did being from Manasseh mean I was a little more special than other members of the Church?

Maybe it just meant I might never fully fit in.

I thought about Bishop Harrington's displeasure with me.

I'd suggest the rest of the blessing continued in a mostly routine manner, only I didn't know enough about the content of anyone else's blessings to conclude that with any certainty. I was surprised, though, when Brother Mason paused and then declared, "You will have the gift of prophecy. You will be able to foresee the future."

That couldn't be in the standard blessing. Was I destined to become president of the Church? Of course, even apostles were seers and revelators. Maybe even the seventies. Perhaps all it meant, though, was that I'd be a stake patriarch myself one day. In any event, it was exciting. Maybe getting my blessing wasn't such a bad idea, after all.

"You must never share your blessing with anyone other than your wife," Brother Mason admonished me when he'd finished, "and not even with her until after you're married."

"Will all these things really happen to me?" I asked. There was talk of my baptizing "dozens" during my mission, which would make me a superstar if I did serve in the Czech Republic.

"If you obey the commandments," the patriarch replied. "Everything in your blessing is contingent on you remaining faithful."

"Everything?" Would I be adopted by a less valiant tribe, I wondered, if I strayed?

"Even the spirits assigned to be your children will be sent to another family if you leave the Church."

I frowned. "So I'll get spirits the Lord doesn't care about as much?"

Brother Mason looked at me a long moment. Then he said, a little stiffly, "Let's join the others in the living room." Giving a blessing, I noticed, seemed to be quite an emotional strain. I wondered how much harder it must be to function as the Lord's mouthpiece for the whole Church.

Perhaps, then, I didn't want to be completely faithful. I wasn't sure I wanted the responsibility of prophecy. I'd seen on the news that the Russians had hacked into U.S. nuclear power plants and could shut them down at will or even send them into a meltdown. What would happen if I foresaw such an incident and reported it to Homeland Security ahead of time?

I'd be written off as a crackpot or, if the unthinkable happened, I'd be sent to prison for working with the Russians. In the minds of investigators, how else could I know what our enemies were up to?

Perhaps that was why the Prophet never warned the government about 9/11 or other such incidents.

But what good was it to know the future if you couldn't do anything about it?

"How'd it go?" Dad asked on the drive home.

"Okay, I guess."

"Just okay?"

"I'm supposed to have four more kids than I planned to have."

Dad laughed. "And how many is that?"

I could hardly tell him I didn't want to have *any* children. It sounded so selfish. I just felt I could better contribute to the world in other ways. "I'm not supposed to say."

Dad chuckled. "Okay, okay. Anything else?"

Unfortunately, Brother Mason had said nothing about where I might serve my mission, only that I needed to go on one. The one thing he said about my career was, "You'll learn to love your work, knowing you made the right decision to choose responsibility over fanciful dreams." It certainly didn't sound like he wanted me performing in a symphony.

My friends had hinted they'd been promised to live long enough to witness the Second Coming. It reminded me of the way the apostles hinted they'd seen Jesus Christ in person, though they technically never said so. But my blessing hadn't mentioned anything at all about still being alive when the Millennium started. Instead, I'd been told, "You'll live long enough to see the City of Enoch return to the Earth."

Was that normal?

My Sunday School teacher had suggested that the Gulf of Mexico was formed when the City of Enoch was taken up into heaven thousands of years ago. Seemed like an awfully big city to me, especially for Biblical times. Even Tokyo wasn't that large today.

"Nothing worth mentioning," I said.

Dad reached over and patted my leg. "Don't worry, son. Every time you read it, you'll see things you missed before."

"Thanks, Dad."

"Now let me tell you a joke I heard from Sister Mason."

I should have seen that coming.

Over the next couple of weeks, Devin and Heather tried to get me to reveal what my blessing promised but were no more forthcoming with their own, so I stayed mute as well. In Seminary, we learned about King Benjamin. In Young Men's we shot rifles at a shooting range. I avoided a YM/YW dance in the gym.

But I couldn't avoid Bishop Harrington. A few weeks after I received my Patriarchal Blessing, months before I was due back in the bishop's office, he demanded I return. "Are you ready to confess now?" he asked after a few preliminaries, his lips pressed together.

I felt a flash of inspiration, revelation perhaps. I understood for the first time why suspects sometimes gave a false confession. I remembered the 1936 case of Brown v. Mississippi that we'd studied in History, where three Black men were beaten and tortured until they confessed to killing a white man.

Not that bishops' interviews were quite that grueling. I blushed, embarrassed I'd even made the comparison.

"Yes," I said, noting Bishop Harrington's triumphant smile. "After you told me every boy did it, I decided I'd better try it out. So I've been masturbating once a week ever since."

The bishop's mouth fell open, but he managed to shut it quickly. "Well, stop it!" he said, wagging his finger at me.

I nodded. "I think that's best," I agreed. "I'll stop."

Bishop Harrington's eyes narrowed. "Just like that?" He snapped his fingers.

"You want me to take my time stopping?" I asked in confusion.

"No! Stop it now!"

"Okay."

"Craig," Bishop Harrington said wearily, "you're a hard case. But I promise you, I'm harder."

The next few weeks passed by smoothly enough. In Chemistry, we did some more titrations. In History, we learned about the McCarthy hearings. Then in English class, we read "Young Goodman Brown." When Mrs. Moore said, "So we really never know if Goodman Brown saw all those witches or not," I raised my hand. "Yes, Craig?"

"Of course we know," I said. "There's no such thing as witches. At least not the kind that can do the things he saw."

"Do we really know that, Craig?" Mrs. Moore looked at me with a patronizing smile.

"Yes, we do. Believing something crazy doesn't make it true."

"Oh, Craig, you have so much to learn about literature."

I frowned. What did that have to do with the price of cureloms?

In Band, we learned an instrumental version of "Yorktown" from the play *Hamilton*, quite fun. We also learned an arrangement of a difficult violin concerto by Tchaikovsky, though since I wasn't playing the violin, my part wasn't as hard as I'd have liked. I needed more pieces that might help me win a scholarship at a good conservatory.

I practiced my horn at least an hour every afternoon and the trumpet and piccolo maybe fifteen minutes apiece. I worked Saturdays at the only second-hand musical instrument store in town, so I'd have first dibs on any incoming instrument, and maybe the money to buy it. If I could become halfway competent on the trumpet and piccolo by the end of the school year, I could try to learn another two instruments my senior year.

I needed a strong college application. I could probably throw in another relatively easy instrument even now. The cymbals? Something else? I'd have to ask my band director for suggestions.

I'd need to attend whatever school accepted me for at least a year before I left on my mission or risk losing everything after two years away. Dad kept saying, "Mission first, young man. Our number one priority is always Heavenly Father." Then he'd always tell me the same joke, where the punch line was one third of the host of heaven being cast out with Satan. Funny.

Leaving on missions at nineteen had been the norm for decades, but now it was a sin.

When Dad saw me bring home yet another instrument from work, he took me into his office for a one-on-one. "Craig, I've been very patient with you and given you your space. But you're abusing that freedom, and now it looks like you're becoming addicted."

I had to admit, my passion for music seemed to be increasing all the time. "Is being addicted to learning a bad thing?" I asked.

"It is when what you're learning isn't productive, and when it takes time away from learning more important things."

"I'm making straight A's," I said. I thought it best not to tell him how close I'd come to making a B this term in English.

"Just think how much more productive it would be to learn Spanish. You might be sent to one of those high-baptism missions in South America. Or you could learn French. Lots of African countries use French, and the Church baptizes lots of people in those countries."

"I'm studying Czech, Dad. You know that."

"And how many people do you think you'll baptize in Czechoslovakia?"

"The Czech Republic."

"Son," Dad said softly, putting his hand on my arm, "you're going to lose your testimony if you don't put more emphasis on spiritual goals." He shook his head. "A testimony is a fragile thing. Just because you have one now doesn't mean it'll always be there." Now he squeezed my arm. "A testimony is as hard to hold as a moonbeam. It's something you have to recapture every day of your life."

I frowned. "You mean, it can't survive in the sunlight?"

Dad leaned back, removing his hand from my arm. "I don't want to hear from your mom that you've been practicing music for more than half an hour every afternoon."

I bit my lip to keep from "talking back," but I did manage to say carefully, "I'm trying to get a scholarship, Dad. Wouldn't it be great not to have to pay my college tuition?"

"Young man, I don't have to pay it at all if you're going to be difficult."

I nodded, seeing my future slip away. Being taken care of by one's parents was great in most ways, but on another level, we were awfully similar to indentured servants. "Okay, Dad. I'll start studying French, too."

Dad smiled. "That's my boy." He then told a joke about the Prodigal Son, but I didn't pay much attention. I was thinking instead about where in the world I could go to keep practicing my playing without getting caught.

I could probably do it in one of the rooms at work, but that would mean needing to explain to my folks where I was going and why I wasn't getting paid for it. Still, what would my future look like if there was no music in it? The question was too terrifying to contemplate.

The biggest issue was that I just didn't understand the problem. I was a good kid. Everyone was acting as if I was a delinquent. I must be missing something. I supposed even bad kids thought they were good. Donald Trump thought he was good, didn't he?

Speaking of kids.

Dad never found jokes about the President funny. He was hoping to vote for the man a second time.

Dad stood now and motioned me toward his office door. As I walked out, he said to my back, "I don't want you going to band camp this summer. There's a two-week missionary training camp for teens I want you to attend instead. It's to help reduce the number of missionaries who come home early from their mission."

I stopped in my tracks for a second, mumbled, "Sure, Dad," as convincingly as possible, and kept walking.

A few days later, Devin tried to show me a porn magazine he'd "found," but I suggested we ride our bikes instead. I needed my mind to be clearer than ever right now. Then Heather asked if she and I could go out for ice cream sometime. I said only if Devin and Arlene could come along. She agreed to the terms. After she kissed me at the end of the date, I told her we should just stick to seeing each other at church for the time being.

The following Sunday, I was called in to the bishop's office yet again. "We have a serious problem, Craig," Bishop Harrington said heavily.

"What's wrong?" I asked. Had someone complained about the way I conducted myself as Seminary class president?

"It's come to my attention you don't like girls."

"Excuse me?"

"And people have told me they've heard you boasting about 'playing the mouth organ.'" Bishop Harrington took a deep breath. "Craig, are you giving other boys blow jobs?"

My mouth fell open, but as I was afraid that would appear to be a confession, I closed it again quickly. "You can't be serious," I said.

"I'm as serious as the curse of Cain."

"Bishop, I'm learning the harmonica. I just started."

"Don't lie to me, young man. I want the truth."

I felt eerily compelled to shout out a famous Jack Nicholson line but suppressed the urge. Looking into my bishop's earnest face, though, I foresaw my future with a new clarity. A lifetime of interviews alone with various priesthood leaders made Outer Darkness look attractive.

Why witches were unbelievable when evil spirits cast into swine were real, I didn't know. Why was seeing a devil on a lonely country road less likely than waiting anxiously for an entire city to descend from the sky?

Why in the world, I wondered, did we believe an everyday businessman had a personal conduit to heaven? And if such a man could really have one, then why couldn't I?

I stood up.

"Where do you think you're going, young man?"

I looked at the bishop calmly. His hands tensed and his back hunched as if he were ready to spring to his feet. I wanted to say "Home to masturbate" but didn't.

Instead, I worked up my best General Conference voice and answered. "Even perfectly sane people can believe completely crazy things sometimes."

"What's *that* supposed to mean?"

But I walked out of his office without another word.

Books by Johnny Townsend

Thanks for reading! If you enjoyed this book, could you please take a few minutes to write a review online? Reviews are helpful both to me as an author and to other readers, so we'd all sincerely appreciate your writing one! And if you did enjoy the book, here are some others I've written you might want to look up:

Mormon Underwear

Zombies for Jesus

A Gay Mormon Missionary in Pompeii

The Golem of Rabbi Loew

Marginal Mormons

Gay Gaslighting

Going-Out-Of-Religion Sale

Escape from Zion

Gayrabian Nights

Missionaries Make the Best Companions

Invasion of the Spirit Snatchers

Sexual Solidarity

The Washing of Brains

Mormon Misfits

Sins of the Saints

The Last Days Linger

The Mysterious Madness of Mormons

Human Compassion for Beginners

Out of the Missionary's Closet

Breaking the Promise of the Promised Land

Am I My Planet's Keeper?

Have Your Cum and Eat It, Too

Strangers with Benefits

Constructing Equity

Wake Up and Smell the Missionaries

Racism by Proxy

Orgy at the STD Clinic

Please Evacuate

Recommended Daily Humanity

The Camper Killings

An Eternity of Mirrors: Best Short Stories of Johnny Townsend

Kinky Quilts: Patchwork Designs for Gay Men

Inferno in the French Quarter: The UpStairs Lounge Fire

Latter-Gay Saints: An Anthology of Gay Mormon Fiction (co-editor)

Available from your favorite online or neighborhood bookstore.

Wondering what some of those other books are about? Read on!

Invasion of the Spirit Snatchers

During the Apocalypse, a group of Mormon survivors in Hurricane, Utah gather in the home of the Relief Society president, telling stories to pass the time as they ration their food storage and await the Second Coming. But this is no ordinary group of Mormons—or perhaps it is. They are the faithful, feminist, gay, apostate, and repentant, all working together to help each other through the darkest days any of them have yet seen.

Gayrabian Nights

Gayrabian Nights is a twist on the well-known classic, *1001 Arabian Nights*, in which Scheherazade, under the threat of death if she ceases to captivate King Shahryar's attention, enchants him through a series of mysterious, adventurous, and romantic tales.

In this variation, a male escort, invited to the hotel room of a closeted, homophobic Mormon senator, learns that the man is poised to vote on a piece of anti-gay legislation the following morning. To prevent him from sleeping, so that the exhausted senator will miss casting his vote on the Senate floor, the escort entertains him with stories of homophobia, celibacy, mixed orientation marriages, reparative therapy, coming out, first love, gay marriage, and long-term successful gay relationships.

The escort crafts the stories to give the senator a crash course in gay culture and sensibilities, hoping to bring the man closer to accepting his own sexual orientation.

Inferno in the French Quarter: The UpStairs Lounge Fire

On Gay Pride Day in 1973, someone set the entrance to a French Quarter gay bar on fire. In the terrible inferno that followed, thirty-two people lost their lives, including a third of the local congregation of the Metropolitan Community Church, their pastor burning to death halfway out a second-story window as he tried to claw his way to freedom. A mother who'd gone to the bar with her two gay sons died alongside them. A man who'd helped his friend escape first was found dead near the fire escape. Two children waited outside a movie theater across town for a father and "uncle" who would never pick them up. During this era of rampant homophobia, several families refused to claim the bodies, and many churches refused to bury the dead.

Author Johnny Townsend pored through old records and tracked down survivors of the fire as well as relatives and friends of those killed to compile this fascinating account of a forgotten moment in gay history.

A Gay Mormon Missionary in Pompeii

What is a gay Mormon missionary doing in Italy? He is trying to save his own soul as well as the souls of others. In these tales chronicling the two-year mission of Robert Anderson, we see a young man tormented by his inability to be the man the Church says he should be. In addition to his personal hell, Anderson faces a major earthquake, organized crime, a serious bus accident, and much more. He copes with horrendous mission leaders and his own suicidal tendencies. But one day, he meets another missionary who loves him, and his world changes forever.

Missionaries Make the Best Companions

What lies behind the freshly scrubbed façades of the Mormon missionaries we see about town? In these stories, an ex-Mormon tries to seduce a faithful elder by showing him increasingly suggestive movies. A sister missionary fulfills her community service requirement by babysitting for a prostitute. Two elders break their mission rules by venturing into the forbidden French Quarter. A senior missionary couple try to reactivate lapsed members while their own family falls apart back home. A young man hopes that serving a second full-time mission will lead him up the Church hierarchy. Two bored missionaries decide to make a little extra money moonlighting in a male stripper club. Two frustrated elders find an acceptable way to masturbate—by donating to a Fertility Clinic. A lonely man searches for the favorite companion he hasn't seen in thirty years.

The Golem of Rabbi Loew

Jacob and Esau Cohen are the closest of brothers. In fact, they're lovers. A doctor tries to combine canine genes with those of Jews, to improve their chances of surviving a hostile world. A Talmudic scholar dates an escort. A scientist tries to develop the "God spot" in the brains of his patients in hopes of creating a messiah.

A Jew-by-Choice navigates Jewish/Muslim relations during Pesach. A gay Lubavitcher dating a Catholic is attacked and left for dead but becomes a police officer in response. The Golem of Prague is really Rabbi Loew's secret lover.

While some of the Jews in Townsend's book are Orthodox, this collection of Jewish stories most certainly is not.

Am I My Planet's Keeper?

Global Warming. Climate Change. Climate Crisis. Climate Emergency. Whatever label we use, we are facing one of the greatest challenges to the survival of life as we know it.

But while addressing greenhouse gases is perhaps our most urgent need, it's not our only task. We must also address toxic waste, pollution, habitat destruction, and our other contributions to the world's sixth mass extinction event.

In order to do that, we must simultaneously address the unmet human needs that keep us distracted from deeper engagement in stabilizing our climate: moderating economic inequality, guaranteeing healthcare to all, and ensuring education for everyone.

And to accomplish *that*, we must unite to combat the monied forces that use fear, prejudice, and misinformation to manipulate us.

It's a daunting task. But success is our only option.

Wake Up and Smell the Missionaries

Two Mormon missionaries in Italy discover they share the same rare ability—both can emit pheromones on demand. At first, they playfully compete in the hills of Frascati to see who can tempt "investigators" most. But soon they're targeting each other non-stop.

Can two immature young men learn to control their "superpower" to live a normal life…and develop genuine love? Even as their relationship is threatened by the attentions of another man?

They seem just on the verge of success when a massive earthquake leaves them trapped under the rubble of their apartment in Castellammare.

With night falling and temperatures dropping, can they dig themselves out in time to save themselves? And will their injuries destroy the ability that brought them together in the first place?

Orgy at the STD Clinic

Todd Tillotson is struggling to move on after his husband is killed in a hit and run attack a year earlier during a Black Lives Matter protest in Seattle.

In this novel set entirely on public transportation, we watch as Todd, isolated throughout the pandemic, battles desperation in his attempt to safely reconnect with the world.

Will he find love again, even casual friendship, or simply end up another crazy old man on the bus?

Things don't look good until a man whose face he can't even see sits down beside him despite the raging variants.

And asks him a question that will change his life.

Please Evacuate

A gay, partygoing New Yorker unconcerned about the future or the unsustainability of capitalism is hit by a truck and thrust into a straight man's body half a continent away. As Hunter tries to figure out what's happening, he's caught up in another disaster, a wildfire sweeping through a Colorado community, the flames overtaking him and several schoolchildren as they flee.

When he awakens, Hunter finds himself in the body of yet another man, this time in northern Italy, a former missionary about to marry a young Mormon woman. Still piecing together this new reality, and beginning to embrace his latest identity, Hunter fights for his life in a devastating flash flood along with his wife *and* his new husband.

He's an aging worker in drought-stricken Texas, a nurse at an assisted living facility in the direct path of a hurricane, an advocate for the unhoused during a freak Seattle blizzard.

We watch as Hunter is plunged into life after life, finally recognizing the futility of only looking out for #1 and understanding the part he must play in addressing the global climate crisis...if he ever gets another chance.

Recommended Daily Humanity

A checklist of human rights must include basic housing, universal healthcare, equitable funding for public schools, and tuition-free college and vocational training.

In addition to the basics, though, we need much more to fully thrive. Subsidized childcare, universal pre-K, a universal basic income, subsidized high-speed internet, net neutrality, fare-free public transit (plus *more* public transit), and medically assisted death for the terminally ill who want it.

None of this will matter, though, if we neglect to address the rapidly worsening climate crisis.

Sound expensive? It is.

But not as expensive as refusing to implement these changes. The cost of climate disasters each year has grown to staggering figures. And the cost of social and political upheaval from not meeting the needs of suffering workers, families, and individuals may surpass even that.

It's best we understand that the vast sums required to enact meaningful change are an investment which will pay off not only in some indeterminate future but in fact almost immediately. And without these adjustments to our lifestyles and values, there may very well not be a future capable of sustaining freedom and democracy…or even civilization itself.

The Camper Killings

When a homeless man is found murdered a few blocks from Morgan Beylerian's house in south Seattle, everyone seems to consider the body just so much additional trash to be cleared from the neighborhood. But Morgan liked the guy. They used to chat when Morgan brought Nick groceries once a week.

And the brutal way the man was killed reminds Morgan of their shared Mormon heritage, back when the faithful agreed to have their throats slit if they ever revealed temple secrets.

Did Nick's former wife take action when her ex-husband refused to grant a temple divorce? Did his murder have something to do with the public accusations that brought an end to his promising career?

Morgan does his best to investigate when no one else seems to care, but it isn't easy as a man living paycheck to paycheck himself, only able to pursue his investigation via public transit.

As he continues his search for the killer, Morgan's friends withdraw and his husband threatens to leave. When another homeless man is killed and Morgan is accused of the crime, things look even bleaker.

But his troubles aren't over yet.

Will Morgan find the killer before the killer finds him?

What Readers Have Said

Townsend's stories are "a gay *Portnoy's Complaint* of Mormonism. Salacious, sweet, sad, insightful, insulting, religiously ethnic, quirky-faithful, and funny."

D. Michael Quinn, author of *The Mormon Hierarchy: Origins of Power*

"Told from a believably conversational first-person perspective, [*A Gay Mormon Missionary in Pompeii*'s] novelistic focus on Anderson's journey to thoughtful self-acceptance allows for greater character development than often seen in short stories, which makes this well-paced work rich and satisfying, and one of Townsend's strongest. An extremely important contribution to the field of Mormon fiction." Named to Kirkus Reviews' Best of 2011.

Kirkus Reviews

"The thirteen stories in *Mormon Underwear* capture this struggle [between Mormonism and homosexuality] with humor, sadness, insight, and sometimes shocking details....*Mormon Underwear* provides compelling stories, literally from the inside-out."

Niki D'Andrea, *Phoenix New Times*

"Townsend's lively writing style and engaging characters [in *Zombies for Jesus*] make for stories which force us to wake up, smell the (prohibited) coffee, and review our attitudes with regard to reading dogma so doggedly. These are tales which revel in the individual tics and quirks which make us human, Mormon or not, gay or not…"

A.J. Kirby, *The Short Review*

"The Rift," from *A Gay Mormon Missionary in Pompeii*, is a "fascinating tale of an untenable situation…a *tour de force*."

David Lenson, editor, *The Massachusetts Review*

"Pronouncing the Apostrophe," from *The Golem of Rabbi Loew*, is "quiet and revealing, an intriguing tale…"

Sima Rabinowitz, Literary Magazine Review, *NewPages.com*

The Circumcision of God is "a collection of short stories that consider the imperfect, silenced majority of Mormons, who may in fact be [the Church's] best hope….[The book leaves] readers regretting the church's willingness to marginalize those who best exemplify its ideals: those who love fiercely despite all obstacles, who brave challenges at great personal risk and who always choose the hard, higher road."

Kirkus Reviews

In *Mormon Fairy Tales*, Johnny Townsend displays "both a wicked sense of irony and a deep well of compassion."

Kel Munger, *Sacramento News and Review*

Zombies for Jesus is "eerie, erotic, and magical."

Publishers Weekly

"While [Townsend's] many touching vignettes draw deeply from Mormon mythology, history, spirituality and culture, [*Mormon Fairy Tales*] is neither a gaudy act of proselytism nor angry protest literature from an ex-believer. Like all good fiction, his stories are simply about the joys, the hopes and the sorrows of people."

Kirkus Reviews

"In *Inferno in the French Quarter* author Johnny Townsend restores this tragic event [the UpStairs Lounge fire] to its proper place in LGBT history and reminds us that the victims of the blaze were not just 'statistics,' but real people with real lives, families, and friends."

Jesse Monteagudo, *The Bilerico Project*

In *Inferno in the French Quarter*, "Townsend's heart-rending descriptions of the victims…seem to [make them] come alive once more."

Kit Van Cleave, *OutSmart Magazine*

Marginal Mormons is "an irreverent, honest look at life outside the mainstream Mormon Church….Throughout his musings on sin and forgiveness, Townsend beautifully demonstrates his characters' internal, perhaps irreconcilable struggles….Rather than anger and disdain, he offers an honest portrayal of people searching for meaning and community in their lives, regardless of their life choices or secrets." Named to Kirkus Reviews' Best of 2012.

Kirkus Reviews

The stories in *The Mormon Victorian Society* "register the new openness and confidence of gay life in the age of same-sex marriage….What hasn't changed is Townsend's wry, conversational prose, his subtle evocations of character and social dynamics, and his deadpan humor. His warm empathy still glows in this intimate yet clear-eyed engagement with Mormon theology and folkways. Funny, shrewd and finely wrought dissections of the awkward contradictions—and surprising harmonies—between conscience and desire." Named to Kirkus Reviews' Best of 2013.

Kirkus Reviews

"This collection of short stories [*The Mormon Victorian Society*] featuring gay Mormon characters slammed [me] in the face from the first page, wrestled my heart and mind to the floor, and left me panting and wanting more by the end. Johnny Townsend has created so many memorable characters in such few pages. I went weeks thinking about this book. It truly touched me."

Tom Webb, *A Bear on Books*

Dragons of the Book of Mormon is an "entertaining collection….Townsend's prose is sharp, clear, and easy to read, and his characters are well rendered…"

Publishers Weekly

"The pre-eminent documenter of alternative Mormon lifestyles…Townsend has a deep understanding of his characters, and his limpid prose, dry humor and well-grounded (occasionally magical) realism make their spiritual conundrums both compelling and entertaining. [*Dragons of the Book of Mormon* is] [a]nother of Townsend's critical but affectionate and absorbing tours of Mormon discontent." Named to Kirkus Reviews' Best of 2014.

Kirkus Reviews

In *Gayrabian Nights*, "Townsend's prose is always limpid and evocative, and…he finds real drama and emotional depth in the most ordinary of lives."

Kirkus Reviews

Gayrabian Nights is a "complex revelation of how seriously soul damaging the denial of the true self can be."

Ryan Rhodes, author of *Free Electricity*

Gayrabian Nights "was easily the most original book I've read all year. Funny, touching, topical, and thoroughly enjoyable."

Rainbow Awards

Lying for the Lord is "one of the most gripping books that I've picked up for quite a while. I love the author's writing style, alternately cynical, humorous, biting, scathing, poignant, and touching…. This is the third book of his that I've read, and all are equally engaging. These are stories that need to be told, and the author does it in just the right way."

Heidi Alsop, *Ex-Mormon Foundation Board Member*

In *Lying for the Lord*, Townsend "gets under the skin of his characters to reveal their complexity and conflicts....shrewd, evocative [and] wryly humorous."

Kirkus Reviews

In *Missionaries Make the Best Companions*, "the author treats the clash between religious dogma and liberal humanism with vivid realism, sly humor, and subtle feeling as his characters try to figure out their true missions in life. Another of Townsend's rich dissections of Mormon failures and uncertainties..." Named to Kirkus Reviews' Best of 2015.

Kirkus Reviews

In *Invasion of the Spirit Snatchers*, "Townsend, a confident and practiced storyteller, skewers the hypocrisies and eccentricities of his characters with precision and affection. The outlandish framing narrative is the most consistent source of shock and humor, but the stories do much to ground the reader in the world—or former world—of the characters....A funny, charming tale about a group of Mormons facing the end of the world."

Kirkus Reviews

"Townsend's collection [*The Washing of Brains*] once again displays his limpid, naturalistic prose, skillful narrative chops, and his subtle insights into psychology...Well-crafted dispatches on the clash between religion and self-fulfillment..."

Kirkus Reviews

"While the author is generally at his best when working as a satirist, there are some fine, understated touches in these tales [*The Last Days Linger*] that will likely affect readers in subtle ways....readers should come away impressed by the deep empathy he shows for all his characters—even the homophobic ones."

Kirkus Reviews

"Written in a conversational style that often uses stories and personal anecdotes to reveal larger truths, this immensely approachable book [*Racism by Proxy*] skillfully serves its intended audience of White readers grappling with complex questions regarding race, history, and identity. The author's frequent references to the Church of Jesus Christ of Latter-day Saints may be too niche for readers unfamiliar with its idiosyncrasies, but Townsend generally strikes a perfect balance of humor, introspection, and reasoned arguments that will engage even skeptical readers."

Kirkus Reviews

Orgy at the STD Clinic portrays "an all-too real scenario that Townsend skewers to wincingly accurate proportions...[with] instant classic moments courtesy of his punchy, sassy, sexy lead character..."

Jim Piechota, *Bay Area Reporter*

Orgy at the STD Clinic is "…a triumph of humane sensibility. A richly textured saga that brilliantly captures the fraying social fabric of contemporary life." Named to Kirkus Reviews' Best Indie Books of 2022.

Kirkus Reviews

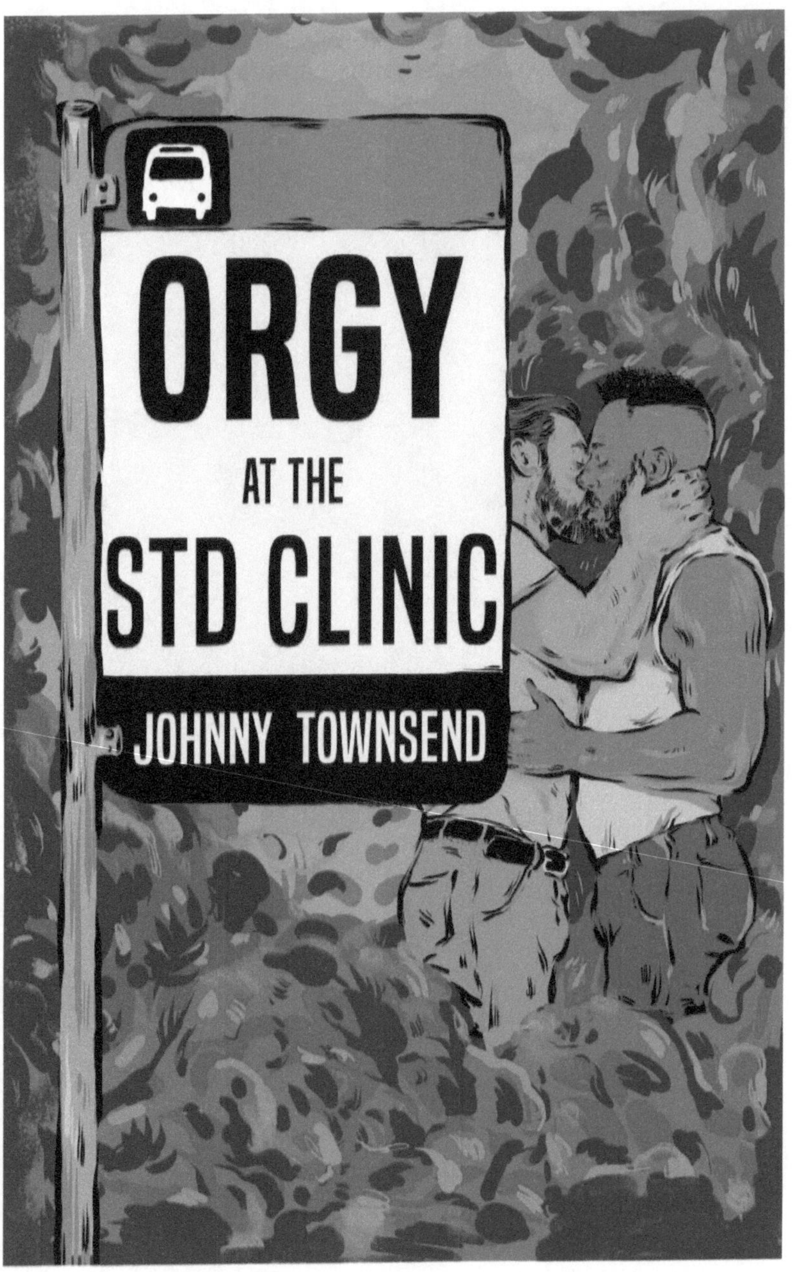

ORGY
AT THE
STD CLINIC
JOHNNY TOWNSEND

HAVE YOUR CUM AND EAT IT, TOO
JOHNNY TOWNSEND

Going-Out-Of-
Religion Sale
JOHNNY TOWNSEND